Praise for Susan Berliner's first novel, *DUST*

"Susan Berliner gives us an amazing mysterious supernatural story in *Dust*. It intrigues and holds the readers' attention, while pulling them in and not letting them put it down."

—*Night Owl Reviews* (Top Pick)

"*Dust* is an excellent first attempt for this new author. I very much enjoyed this actioned scifi/mystery/thriller...Look out Stephen King, this lady may be on your tail!"

—Dottie Taylor, *Tink's Place*

"*Dust* picks you up and takes you on a whirlwind ride, pun intended, and doesn't let you go until the final climax. The characters and settings are believable and the bantering between Karen and Jerry makes you forget these are fictional characters and makes you root for them in their quest to find the dust's weakness...It's a great piece of escapist fiction and a book to easily get lost in."

—Patricia Lane

"Susan Berliner's first novel is filled with drama, laughter, and engaging characters. I immediately connected with Karen and Jerry, a unique couple faced with a mind-boggling swirl of colorful dust...As a high school English teacher, I plan to use this captivating novel with my students this year. I give *DUST* an A+!"

—Brittany Mott

"I was able to read this book in its entirety within just a few hours, which added to its cinematic qualities; it was like watching a movie in the afternoon...The book is fast-paced, and does not dwell on technical jargon in order to explain the paranormal events or the entity, which I found refreshing...The language in the book is relatively simple and casual, easy to read, and doesn't contain much in the way of profanity, so it can be enjoyed by a wide age-group spectrum. I have quickly become a fan of this author, and look forward to her next work."

—Andy S. Adams

PEACHWOOD LAKE

PEACHWOOD LAKE

by Susan Berliner

Published by SRB Books

ISBN: 978-0-9839401-0-4
ISBN: 978-0-9839401-1-1

Cover design and book layout by Dianne and Danielle Paulet
Author's photo by Rachel Leib Photography

Published November, 2011

Printed in the United States of America

This book is dedicated to my children—David, Meredith, and Paul. Thanks so much for your valuable suggestions and continued support.

And a special thanks to my husband, Larry, for always being there for me.

AUTHOR'S NOTE

Each summer, a bizarre ritual takes place in Florida's Suwannee River: Large bony fish—gulf sturgeons—jump high out of the water and sometimes hit hapless boaters, breaking their arms or shattering their legs, and knocking them unconscious. According to scientists, these fish aren't mean and don't intentionally try to hurt people. But no one can figure out why they jump.

After reading about this strange annual occurrence, I wondered: What might happen if a far more ferocious jumping fish than the Florida sturgeon seized control of a tranquil lake and viciously attacked boaters and swimmers—with the sole purpose of killing them?

Peachwood Lake answers that question.

CHAPTER 1

Ode to a Clear Summer Day
The sun brightens the blue sky.
Its hot rays warm my naked shoulder...

"That really sucks," Kady Gonzalez muttered as she angrily crossed out the newly-written lines with heavy pencil slashes, nearly gouging through to the next page of her spiral notebook.

Kady sat on the unused boat dock behind the small cottage she and her father rented on Peachwood Lake. At eleven o'clock on a mid-July Monday morning in 2009, it was beautiful outside—even though Kady hadn't been able to transpose that observation into acceptable poetry. The day wasn't unbearably hot yet and it promised to be far less muggy than usual.

"How'm I ever gonna be a writer if I can't even write a short poem?" she mumbled, staring at her now indecipherable words.

Her seventh-grade English teacher had said she had talent. "You've got a good grasp of language and show real promise as a writer," were Mrs. Wilson's exact words. Kady had immediately written down the teacher's statement to preserve it as an inspiration for times like this when she was feeling discouraged. She had dredged up the sentence so many times that she had memorized it.

Unfortunately, Kady didn't like anything she had written so far. But Mrs. Wilson had told her to keep writing and not give up, so she continued creating, and then destroying, poems and short stories.

"I don't have anything better to do anyway," Kady whispered, shifting her attention from her latest ruined page to the tranquil, clear blue-green water of Peachwood Lake.

The sparkling lake was surrounded by about sixty houses, most of them small cottages like hers, converted from summer homes into year-round residences. The lake was also framed by numerous trees and bushes. Strangely, as far as anyone could determine, none of the trees produced peaches. Off to the left, Kady could just barely see the town's small beach and recreation area, a place she never visited. Across from her home, on the far right side of the lake, Fairview Day Camp boasted a much larger beach. Most summer afternoons when she was outside, Kady could hear the sounds of children screaming and laughing as they swam and cavorted in the water.

Sighing deeply, she turned the page of her notebook and tried to come up with an idea for a new poem. Her thoughts were soon interrupted by a loud splashing noise. She scanned the water, but saw no one in the lake. *Who made that sound?* she wondered.

Kady frowned and again studied the peaceful lake. She could see an undulating eddy towards the middle, but nothing else was visible. She picked up her pencil and wrote "Hot Summer...." Then she heard a second splash.

Kady put the pencil on the dock and stood up, focusing on the lake. *Really weird*, she thought as she continued to stare and listen. It was absolutely quiet except for a few intermittent bird chirps. Suddenly, a long fish, covered with segmented pieces of silver, jumped high out of the water and splashed heavily back down.

"Wow!" Kady said aloud. "That was awesome! A jumping fish that looks like it's wearing a suit of armor!" Again she sat, this time crossing her legs as she faced the lake. Then she picked up the pencil, erased the words "Hot Summer," and wrote a new title: "Ode to a Silver Jumping Fish." Sitting on the dock, she started to compose her new poem.

—m—

Marty Urloch finished making his peanut butter sandwich and began assembling his fishing gear. *Great day to be out on the lake*, the retired appliance salesman thought as he packed his favorite bait—carp doughballs—a tasty concoction Marty had prepared especially for the unsuspecting fish. He grabbed a couple of cold cans of beer from the fridge, picked up his fishing rod, reel, and tackle box, and headed to the backyard boat dock.

Marty placed his fishing equipment and food on a small bench while he retrieved a pair of oars from under the rear porch. After securing the oars, he lowered his gear into the rowboat. Then, carefully, he stepped inside, untied the rope, and headed towards the middle of Peachwood Lake.

"Ahhh," Marty murmured as he rowed leisurely towards his favorite fishing location. "Best day of the summer so far." He glanced at the shore and spotted Kady, who lived three houses down the street, sitting on her dock, busily writing. "Hi there, young lady!" he shouted, waving at the girl. "Enjoying the sun?"

Kady looked up from her notebook and nodded. Then, with a smile, she returned her neighbor's wave.

Marty arrived at his preferred fishing spot and carefully rested the oars inside the small boat. As he reached for his fishing rod and doughball bait, he heard a ripple in the water. Turning to see where the noise was coming from, he caught a glimpse of a silvery streak followed by a loud splash. *What the hell fish was that?* he thought. The man sat quietly, but heard no other sound.

Again Marty bent to pick up his fishing gear. This time, he saw a segmented silver fish leap high out of the water and plummet back in. "Strange," he muttered. "Never seen a jumping fish in the lake." He continued preparing his rod, attaching the special bait.

Marty heard yet another noisy splash. Like a sleek silver missile, the jumping fish rammed into the man's face, landing hard on the left side of his cheek before quickly bouncing back into the lake. "Oww," he groaned, putting down his fishing pole and rubbing the injured part of his face. "That damn fish!"

With another warp-speed splash, the brazen fish jumped into the boat again, aiming for Marty's right eye. The man ducked slightly and the creature bit him hard on the forehead. He wiped his head with his hand, saw the blood, and immediately reached for his oars. "I'm gettin' out of here," he murmured.

As Marty started to maneuver the oars, the silver fish leaped up yet again, zooming directly at his neck. Since Marty had both his hands on the oars, he was unable to protect himself as the whizzing fish projectile reached its target. Flashing a mouthful of sharp dagger-like teeth, the charging creature slashed his neck, creating a deep jagged wound.

In great pain, Marty grabbed his bleeding neck and swerved sharply, toppling the boat. Trying to staunch the blood flowing through his throbbing neck with one hand while paddling to stay afloat in the water with the other hand, he shouted "Help me!" desperately hoping his young neighbor on the dock could hear his cries.

Switching to an underwater attack mode, the tenacious fish continued its war on the man, biting his thighs and legs with its razor-sharp teeth. *This can't be happening!* Marty thought as he tried to swim away from the savage creature. Then the silver fish again hurled itself out of the water, hitting him squarely in the face, and the man sank below the surface.

—〰—

Kady was engrossed in composing her new poem when she heard a commotion in the water. Looking up, she saw Mr. Urloch flailing at something in his rowboat. Squinting from the sun, she held her hand over her eyes to get a clearer picture of what was happening.

Her neighbor was fighting with a fish and it looked like that jumping silver fish. It had huge teeth and was biting him! She watched as the man started to row. But then the boat capsized and he tumbled into the water.

"Oh my God!" Kady shouted as she jumped up and ran inside to call the police. Grabbing the kitchen phone, she dialed 911. "There's been a bad accident in the middle of Peachwood Lake," she gasped when the operator answered. "A man was fighting with a fish and his boat turned over and now he's in the water. Please hurry. I think he could be badly hurt." Quickly, she gave the operator her name and address and rushed back outside.

Kady ran to the edge of her dock and scanned the water for Mr. Urloch. While she clearly saw the rowboat undulating softly in the middle of the lake, there was no sign of her neighbor. With tears flowing down her cheeks, she sat down and waited for help to arrive.

—ແ—

Within minutes, Kady heard the whirr of sirens heading down her street. Wiping her eyes, she ran to the front of her house just as a police car pulled up, followed by an ambulance and a small white van with the words "Water Rescue Unit" printed in blue. Two young men dressed in diving gear jumped out of the van and rushed to Kady.

"You called in the emergency?" one of the divers asked as he strode purposefully towards the lake.

"Yes." Kady had to run to keep up with the fast-moving man.

"Show us where you saw him last."

"Mr. Urloch was in the water right in the middle of the lake, near where his boat is." She pointed to the rowboat, which still rocked gently in the water.

"Thanks," the man said as he and his companion hurried into the lake. Then, while she watched from the dock, the two men swam rapidly towards the rowboat and dived under the water.

Kady was still staring intently at the lake when she heard footsteps behind her. Turning around, she faced a handsome curly-haired policeman.

The tall, lanky officer stood next to her. "Are you Kady Gonzalez?" he asked.

"Yes. Do you think Mr. Urloch could be okay?"

The young policeman paused. "Honestly, it doesn't look very good," he said, shaking his head sadly. "The man's been in the water at least ten minutes...My name's Officer Malone and, while we're waiting, I'd like to know exactly what you saw happen here." He took a small pad and a pen from his pants pocket and began writing.

"It was really weird," Kady said. "At first I heard some kind of strange noise...I think Mr. Urloch was fighting with a fish in the boat."

"What do you mean 'fighting with a fish'? Was the fish so big that the man was struggling to get it off his pole?"

"No. That's not what happened." She spoke quietly and gazed at the ground. "I think this fish jumped into his boat. Then it was biting his neck."

"What?" The policeman gave the girl an incredulous look.

"I know it sounds like I'm nuts," Kady said. "But I saw a silver fish jumping high up out of the water just before Mr. Urloch went out in his boat." She bent down and picked up her notebook, which, with all the commotion, she had tossed on the dock. "Look, I even started to write a poem about it." She quickly flipped the pages to "Ode to a Silver Jumping Fish" and pointed to her half-finished poem. "See?"

Officer Malone shook his head in disbelief. "I've lived in Peachwood all my life," he said. "Been swimming and sailing here every summer and I've never seen or heard anybody mention a jumping fish."

"Yeah," Kady agreed. "I'd never seen any fish like that in the lake until today either."

"Do you know if Mr. Urloch is married?" the policeman asked.

"I don't think so. He lives by himself. My dad said Mr. Urloch told him he moved here after he retired so he could spend lots of time fishing."

"Thank you." Officer Malone scribbled something in his pad.

Then he looked up and sighed.

Kady and the policeman stood quietly on the dock watching the two divers search for Marty Urloch. As they waited, the girl heard several voices nearby. On her left, she saw about ten of her neighbors, who must have heard the sirens and seen the emergency vehicles, standing on the grass near the water. Mrs. Winzinski from up the street smiled at her and she nodded to the woman.

—ɯ—

A few minutes later, one of the divers gestured to Officer Malone. "They've found him," the policeman said. With a quick hand wave, he signaled the two EMTs—a young African-American man and an older blonde woman who had been standing near the ambulance—that he needed them. Meanwhile, Officer Malone walked off the dock and headed for the edge of the grass, motioning the congregating people to move back.

The policeman turned to Kady, who had followed him. "I want you to go inside your house now," he said. "This isn't something you should see."

"Please let me stay," she begged. "I won't scream or yell or say anything. I promise."

"Your parents at work?"

"My dad is."

Officer Malone studied the girl. "All right," he finally said. "But if you make a sound, you'll have to leave."

Kady nodded in agreement.

Then, as they both watched, the divers carried Marty Urloch towards the shore and carefully lowered him onto the grass. Although Kady had never seen a dead body before, it was obvious her neighbor was no longer alive. His eyes were open, but they gazed motionlessly upward, not looking at anything. His mouth seemed to have a questioning look, as if he couldn't believe what had happened to him. There was a large gash on his forehead and an even larger jagged slice across his neck. Bite marks covered his cheeks and his exposed arms.

Kady covered her mouth with her right hand to stifle a scream. *What happened out there?* she wondered. *What kind of fish does this?*

As the crowd whispered quietly, she watched the two EMTs put Mr. Urloch's body on a stretcher and carry him to the ambulance.

"Is your father able to get off work?" Officer Malone asked.

Kady was still afraid she would scream if she opened her mouth so she just shook her head.

"Can you at least call him?" the policeman continued.

Kady tried to talk. "Okay," she whispered. But the word came out chokingly and heavy tears started to flow down her cheeks.

Officer Malone put his arm around the young teen. "You wanted to be here, but this is tough for anyone." He spoke in a soft, soothing voice. "Come down to the station with me for the rest of the day till your dad gets home."

"No," Kady murmured, wiping the tears with her palm and hoping they would stop. "I'll be okay." She moved away from the policeman. "I'll go inside and read or watch TV till he comes home."

"And when will that be?"

"A little after five. He works right in town."

"What does he do?"

"He's a data processor for CompuTechno Industries." Kady paused and slowly looked up at the policeman. "My dad gets paid by the hour and he says we really need the money." The tears had finally stopped and her voice no longer sounded quivery.

"You promise you'll call him right now?" Officer Malone persisted.

"Yes," she whispered.

The policeman took his wallet from his pants pocket and pulled out a business card. Then he quickly wrote something on it and handed the card to Kady. "Here," he said. "Take this. My full name's Pete Malone and I wrote down my cell number. If you change your mind or just want to talk, call me."

Kady stared at the ground. Officer Malone gently lifted her chin so that she had to look at him. "Okay?"

"Okay," she murmured.

"Now you go on inside and call your dad," the policeman repeated.

"Yes sir," Kady mumbled. As Officer Malone watched, she slowly walked to the sliding glass door and entered the cottage.

She stepped into the small kitchen, put the card the officer had given her on the counter, and poured a glass of water. After taking a few sips, she picked up the phone and dialed her father's work number.

"Edgar Gonzalez speaking."

"Hi, Dad," Kady began. "I know you don't like me to call, but..."

"What's wrong?"

"Something really bad just happened." She tried not to choke on her words. "Mr. Urloch went out in his rowboat and this jumping fish went after him and then the police and divers came..."

"What do you mean a 'jumping fish went after him'?" her father interrupted.

"I saw this big silver fish jump high out of the water this morning. Then, a few minutes later, I'm pretty sure I saw Mr. Urloch fighting with it."

Edgar was quiet for several moments. "You said something about police and divers," he finally said.

"Yes, when I saw Mr. Urloch fall into the lake, I called the police. The divers pulled him out of the water, but he was already de-de-dea..." She was sobbing too heavily to pronounce the last word clearly.

"Kady, take it easy," her father said quietly. "I'm real sorry you had to see that. Poor Mr. Urloch. He was a good guy." Edgar hesitated before continuing. "Listen, I'm going to tell my boss that I have an emergency and have to go home early. Meanwhile, turn on the TV and find something funny or dumb to watch. Don't think about what you saw. Okay?"

"There's not much funny stuff on TV except stupid cartoons so I'm just gonna try to read."

"I'm sorry, Kady, but my boss just gave me a dirty look so I'm going to hang up and talk to him right now. I'll be home very soon. Bye."

—⟋⟍⟍—

Kady was reading a copy of *Entertainment Weekly* and trying to forget about Mr. Urloch and the fish when the phone rang. She answered it and said "Hello."

"Hi," said a pleasant male voice. "Is this Katy Gonzalez?"

"Yes, but it's 'Kady' with a 'd.'" She was forever correcting people about the spelling of her name.

"Sorry, Kady. I'm Jake Ellsbury from the *County Courier* and I'm writing a story about what happened in Peachwood Lake earlier today. I'd like to ask you a couple of questions." He paused. "How old are you?"

"Thirteen."

"You saw the accident?"

"Yes," she whispered.

"Just what did you see?"

"Like I told Officer Malone," she said, talking quickly, "I heard noise in the water and when I looked up, I saw Mr. Urloch fighting with a big silver fish."

"A shark?"

"No, I'm sure it wasn't a shark. It was just a long silver fish with lots of big pointy teeth."

"The fish was in the man's boat?"

"Yes."

"Still on his fishing rod?"

"No, it wasn't like that." Kady was getting annoyed. She kept telling people what she had seen, but no one believed her. "Mr. Urloch didn't catch that fish. I think the fish jumped into his boat."

The reporter was quiet. "You saw this fish jump into the man's boat?" he finally asked.

"No, I didn't see that. But I saw the same kind of fish jumping high out of the water just before Mr. Urloch went out fishing in his boat.

I'm sorry, but that's all I saw. Goodbye." Before the reporter could ask another question, she hung up.

"Hi, Kady. I'm home!"

The girl lowered the book she had just started reading and looked at the clock on her night table. It was only 2:00 so her dad had left work very soon after their phone conversation. *He must've really been worried*, she thought, jumping off the bed.

"Hi, Dad." Kady walked into the kitchen and gave her father a quick hug.

Edgar Gonzalez, a short man with thinning hair and a slight paunch, held Kady tightly and returned the hug. Then he took two steps back and studied his daughter. Her heavily-lashed eyes were puffy and her wavy dark-brown hair looked unkempt, tumbling freely around her shoulders, not neatly tied in the usual ponytail. "Are you okay?" he asked quietly.

"I guess so," Kady said. "I did like you said and tried not to think about what happened. I was reading a pretty good mystery when you came in."

"I listened to the local news driving home and Mr. Urloch's accident was the main story," Edgar said, looking directly into her brown eyes. "Are you sure you saw a fish jump into that boat and attack him?"

"I didn't actually see the fish jump in, but I know Mr. Urloch was fighting with it in the boat...And it wasn't on any fishing pole."

"Maybe it was on the pole first and fell off."

"No." Kady shook her head vehemently. "It wasn't that kind of fight at all. This fish was really trying to hurt Mr. Urloch." She lowered her head. "When they took him out of the lake, he had big cuts and bite marks all over his body," she whispered.

"You shouldn't have seen that."

"Maybe I should have jumped in and tried to help Mr. Urloch." Kady looked up, teary-eyed. "I'm a real good swimmer."

Edgar waved his forefinger at her. "That's crazy talk, Kady. You did the right thing, calling the police and waiting for them. If you went in the water, you'd probably be dead too. I don't want you going into the lake again until they find that fish and kill it."

He smiled and put his arm around the girl. "Let's not talk about this any more...Have you eaten any lunch?"

Kady shook her head.

"I didn't think so. How about I make you something to eat and then we'll play a Scrabble tournament? Bet I can beat you two out of three!"

Kady grinned. "Okay," she said. "But you know I always win."

CHAPTER 2

Kady swam in the middle of Peachwood Lake. It was a particularly hot summer day and she luxuriated in the coolness of the sparkling clear water. "Ah!" she murmured, turning on her back to catch the sun's rays, closing her eyes, and resting. Then, unexpectedly, she heard a loud splash behind her.

As she flipped onto her stomach and searched for the source of the noise, a giant silver fish leaped about twenty feet in front of her and headed in her direction. She saw that it had unbelievably huge serrated teeth. The fish swam directly towards her, grinding its sharp teeth and making an incredibly loud buzzing noise. Swimming as fast as she could, she tried to get away from the monstrous creature, but the fish was much quicker. When it reached her, Kady realized her pursuer wasn't a fish at all—it was a gigantic silver chainsaw. She was totally out of breath, unable to swim anymore, as the fish-chainsaw gnashed its massive teeth and began to chop off her head...

"No!" Kady screamed, opening her eyes and sitting up in bed. She wiped the sweat off her neck and took a deep breath, hoping her scream hadn't awakened her father. She looked at her clock and saw the luminous dial glowing 3:20. Too wound up to go back to sleep, she turned on her reading light and reached for the mystery novel.

—ɯ—

"Good morning, Kady," Edgar said, putting his coffee mug on the table and smiling at his daughter as she entered the kitchen. "Did you sleep well?"

"No," Kady said, sitting next to him. "I had a horrible nightmare. I dreamt that I was swimming in the lake and the jumping fish I saw yesterday was really a giant chainsaw and it was starting to cut off my head..."

Edgar shook his head and sighed. "I was afraid something like that would happen after what you saw at the lake...You want some breakfast before I have to run?"

"No, that's okay, Dad. I'm not really hungry right now. I'll eat something later." Kady glanced at the folded, unopened newspaper on the table. They couldn't afford a computer or cable TV, but her father wanted to know what was happening in town so he had "splurged" on a subscription to the *County Courier*. "Is that today's paper? Remember I told you a reporter called me yesterday and said he was writing a story about Mr. Urloch's accident." She reached for the paper. "Can I look?"

Edgar grabbed the newspaper and held it away from her. "After what you just told me, I don't think you should."

"I'll be fine," Kady insisted. "It was just a dream."

Reluctantly, he handed the paper to his daughter who opened it to the front page. The headline, in heavy black type, read: "**KILLER FISH IN PEACHWOOD LAKE?**" Kady scanned the article and found she was mentioned as the person who had called in the emergency and seen the fish.

"Oh crap," she said angrily.

"What's wrong?"

"I even spelled my name for him and he still wrote 'Katy' with a 't.'"

Edgar smiled softly. "That should be your biggest problem."

"He spoke to Mrs. O'Hara too," Kady continued. "I didn't notice her yesterday, but she must have been one of the people standing here and watching when the divers brought Mr. Urloch out of the water."

"What did Mrs. O'Hara say?"

"She said, 'That poor man didn't just drown. Something in the water killed him. He had deep slashes on his neck and head and bite marks everywhere. I'm not going into the lake until they find and kill whatever did this to him!'"

Kady lowered the newspaper and looked at her father. "What do we do now?" she asked.

"Well, I agree with Mrs. O'Hara," Edgar said, standing and walking to his daughter. "We're not going into the water either until they get rid of that fish." He gave the girl a quick hug. "I've got to get to work now. Will you be okay today without going near the lake?"

"Can I still sit on the dock and write my poems?"

Edgar stood quietly considering the question. "I guess that'll be okay," he finally said. "But don't even dip your feet in." Grasping his daughter's hands, he stared directly into her deep brown eyes. "Promise?"

"Promise," Kady agreed, releasing her hands.

"Have a great and peaceful day," Edgar called from the front door, waving goodbye.

"You too, Dad," Kady said, smiling softly. Then she walked to the door and locked it.

—◊—

Kady put her notebook and pencil on the dock and stood up. This morning, she was finding it difficult to create even her usual bad poetry. She moved to the edge of the wooden pier and stared at the malevolent clear water.

"Hey girl, whatcha doin'?" a lilting feminine voice called out behind her. Kady turned around quickly and faced a tall, young African-American woman whose attractive face was framed by masses of tightly-curled black ringlets.

"I'm sorry," the woman continued, jingling one of her large

hoop earrings. "I didn't mean to scare you. But you were standing so damn quietly, I was afraid you were going to jump in." Reaching into her shoulder bag, she took out a business card and handed it to Kady. "Here. I ought to introduce myself. My name is Monique Atchison and I'm with *Weird World Weekly*."

The girl took the card and stared at it, frowning slightly.

"Did you ever hear of us?" Monique asked.

"Uh uh." Kady shook her head.

"Bet you have." The woman wiggled her forefinger. "When you go to the supermarket...All those shitty papers at the check-out counter—the ones with the dumb headlines like 'Three-Armed Man Wins Juggling Contest.'"

Kady pictured a man with three arms juggling a bunch of balls and smiled.

"And that's a real headline from one of last month's papers," Monique said, chuckling. "How about this one: 'Pet Dog Recites Pledge of Allegiance'? I wrote that article a couple of weeks ago. Poodle sounded pretty damn good too."

Kady's face broke into a wide grin and she giggled. Then she looked at the lake, remembered yesterday's tragedy, and quickly became serious again.

Noticing the change in the girl's expression, Monique stopped smiling. "Hey, I know some bad shit just happened here," she said. "But you gotta laugh too." The reporter put her hands on her slim hips and stared at Kady. "You're real pretty when you smile and way too young to frown so much. You're thirteen, right?"

The girl nodded.

"Yeah, that's what they told me. And what's your name, Miss Serious Thirteen?"

"Kady," she mumbled.

"Nice name. How do you spell it?"

"Like Katy, but with a 'd.' Most people don't get it right."

"I bet they don't." Hopping gracefully off the dock, Monique parked her lithe body on the lawn, facing the lake. "Know what I like about my name?" she asked as she pulled out a piece of crabgrass and started ripping it.

Kady sat beside the young woman. "What?" she asked.

"The ending. You know, the end of 'Monique' sounds just like 'eek,' the scary sound they use in comics when someone sees a mouse and screams."

"I never thought about that."

"Why would you? It's not your name." With a chuckle, Monique tossed the torn grass pieces high into the air.

The two of them sat quietly, neither talking, for a long minute. "You're here because of what happened yesterday," Kady finally said, staring at the lawn.

"Of course. We've got people at *Weird World* whose only job is to find out where shit like this is happening. My editor called me early this morning and told me to get my ass down here to check it out."

"Aren't you going to ask me what I saw yesterday?" Kady still gazed at the grass and frowned.

"Not unless there's something you didn't tell the police or the newspaper. Sounds like you're kinda sick of talking about it." Monique opened her large rust-colored leather bag, took out a small notepad, and turned a few pages. "Let's see. My notes say that a thirteen-year-old girl—that would be you—saw a long silver fish jump out of the water in Peachwood Lake and that fish later attacked and killed your neighbor in his rowboat." She looked at the teen. "Is that it?"

The girl nodded and then frowned.

Monique waved her forefinger in front of Kady's face. "You got to stop frowning so much, girl!"

Kady sighed.

"Interview's over," Monique said, tossing the pad into her shoulder bag. "Let's talk about you. So what'cha been doing so far this summer?"

"Not much," the girl whispered.

"Your folks at work?"

"Just my dad."

"It's just you and your dad living here?"

"Yes. My mother left us when I was a baby."

Monique was silent for a few seconds. "I know what that's like," she finally said.

"You do?"

"Yeah. My mama raised me and my two sisters all by herself." The reporter smiled broadly. "And she did a damn fine job." Still smiling, she turned to Kady. "So what do you do all day while your papa's at work?"

"I try to write poetry."

"Want to read me a poem?"

Kady shook her head. "None of them are any good."

"Well keep writing, girl. You'll be surprised. All of a sudden, one day something you write will sound good to you...Maybe it'll even make you smile."

The teen shrugged her shoulders.

"You ever get together with any other kids?"

Kady didn't answer.

"Go over to a friend's house?" Monique continued.

"I don't have any friends." The girl's voice was barely audible.

"Why not? You're kinda cool, even though you're way too serious."

"How would you know?" Kady asked, her voice rising sharply. "You're not thirteen. None of the girls at school want me to hang out with them. They stand around and whisper things about me and make fun of my clothes." She wiped her eyes. "And even if they liked me, I couldn't do stuff with them anyway. I don't have an iPod or a cell phone. What would we do together—sit around and write poems?"

"How about talk about boys?"

"Boys don't like me either," Kady murmured.

"Yeah, I remember." Monique nodded. "It's tough being thirteen. But it will get better, I promise. Just don't keep putting yourself down for not having stuff that costs a lot of money. You'll find friends that won't care about all that shit."

"Not in this town." The girl shook her head.

"Even in this town." The reporter patted Kady's shoulder.

They sat together quietly until Monique spoke again. "Ever think about earning some money of your own? Maybe you could be a babysitter."

"I babysit the boy next door when he comes home from school. But in the summer, Todd goes to day camp."

"Too bad," Monique said sympathetically.

"Yeah." Kady sighed. Then she turned and gazed at the reporter. "So now that you know all about my wonderful life, what're you going to write for your newspaper?"

"Well, all the time we've been sitting here and talking, I've been looking at your lake and I haven't seen any jumping silver fish. Did anyone else but you see the damn thing?"

The girl shook her head. "I don't think so and I only saw it yesterday morning."

"I do believe you saw a weird fish," Monique said, standing and dusting grass off her rear end. "But maybe it was just a freaky, one-time thing. What happened to that man was real terrible. But that's not what *Weird World* is after. Our readers want monsters and aliens—shit like that—and there's not enough of that here for my kind of story." She spread out her hands. "So, right now, no story."

"I'm sorry you wasted your time."

"What do you mean 'wasted' my time? I got to meet you."

"Yeah, what a lucky break." Kady stared at the grass again.

"Girl, you got to stop thinking about yourself that way," Monique said adamantly as she groped inside her enormous bag. "Listen, I know I gave you my card, but in case you lose it, I'm giving you another. I want you to call me—and I don't mean just about that damn fish—at the number I'm circling. It's my cell and the phone is almost always on." She put the card into Kady's hand and enclosed the girl's fingers around it. "And if I don't hear from you, I'll get your number and, you better believe, I *will* be calling you."

The reporter started walking towards the front of the house with Kady following. "Besides, maybe the autopsy of your neighbor will find that a prehistoric monster fish that hasn't been alive for a million years was the killer," Monique said, reaching her car. "Then you better believe I'll be back to write that story." After hugging the girl, she stepped into the red Elantra and looked up at her before closing the door. "Call me," she said. Then Monique turned on the ignition and slowly drove away.

CHAPTER 3

"You're talking to way too many strangers these days," Edgar said as he and Kady ate dinner together Tuesday evening.

"Monique was a lot of fun," Kady said after chewing a piece of grilled chicken. "You'd like her—and it was a lot better than just sitting around and writing my crappy poems."

Edgar sighed. "I'm sorry, Kady. I wish I had the money to send you to camp like Todd."

The girl immediately regretted mentioning how bored she had been. "Hey, it's okay, Dad. I'm too old to go to camp anyway. It's just that it's been so exciting since Mr. Urloch's accident and..." She stopped in mid-sentence. "I mean, I'm really sorry about what happened to him yester..."

"I understand," her father interrupted. "But reporters phoning you and this Monique person even coming to the house to talk to you..."

"I'm big enough to talk to them, Dad. Besides, Monique is my friend. She gave me her card and wants me to call her."

"That's really nice, Kady. But you need to have friends your own age...How old is Monique?"

"She didn't tell me, but I guess she's about twenty-five."

"That's nearly twice your age."

"Yeah, but she's really cool," Kady said, taking another bite of chicken.

—⁓—

Edgar glanced at the kitchen clock as his daughter finished her chocolate ice cream. "It's time for the local news," he said. "Let's see if they mention anything about what happened in Peachwood Lake."

They walked into their cozy living room, Kady snuggling into the small upholstered chair while her father sat on the loveseat and turned on the TV. A handsome blond anchorman was in mid-sentence: "...to Mayor Margaret Turnbull for a statement about the recent death in Peachwood Lake."

The screen shifted to a close-up of the frumpy, middle-aged, former high school math teacher who had been elected mayor of the town of Peachwood last November. "I'd like to begin by saying how deeply sorry I am about yesterday's tragedy in Peachwood Lake," the mayor began. "I've already spoken to Martin Urloch's family." She adjusted her glasses nervously. "Like most Peachwood natives, I have many fond memories of our beautiful waterway. Right now, we don't have many details about exactly how Mr. Urloch died. All we know is that he was killed by something in the lake and one witness saw him grappling with a fish. We are awaiting the results of the autopsy for more definitive information and we should have those results in a few days." Mayor Turnbull again touched her glasses and tilted them.

"In the meantime, I am advising everyone to stay away from Peachwood Lake. Although the lake is not officially closed, since we don't know what really happened, it is far too dangerous right now for swimming or boating. I know that it's summer and businesses depend on Peachwood Lake for income and many residents enjoy it for leisure activities. But until we get rid of whatever killed Martin Urloch, I urge you: Please do not use the lake." Taking off her glasses, the mayor wiped her eyes with her right hand. "I will update you as soon as we find out more. Thank you."

Edgar pressed the "Mute" button on the remote and turned to

Kady. "Anyone who went into the lake after what happened to Mr. Urloch is an idiot."

"Yeah," the girl agreed. "I don't want to watch TV anymore right now. I'm going outside for a little while. I'll take my book with me and read."

"No dipping your feet in the water," Edgar warned.

"I'm not stupid," Kady said, frowning.

"I know, hon. But I'm your father; I worry."

"Hey, Kady!"

Hearing her name being called just as she was about to step onto the dock, Kady turned around and waved to her next-door neighbor, Mark Cimino, sitting on his patio, as the man's six-year-old son caught up to her.

"Hi, Todd. How's everything?"

"I heard Dad tell Mommy that you saw the fish," the little blond-haired boy gasped, completely out of breath. "Did you see it again? The one that killed Mr. Urloch dead?"

"No."

"Wha'did the bad fish do? Tear him into little pieces? Eat him?"

"Where'd you hear that?" Kady asked. "That's not anything like what I saw. Mr. Urloch was fighting with a big fish, but it wasn't eating him." She gave the little boy a questioning look.

"Well, it must be a pretty bad fish 'cause now I can't go into the water anymore."

"That's true," she agreed, nodding her head and gazing at the sparkling lake.

"Today in camp they wouldn't let us go into the lake, not even a little," the boy continued. "And tomorrow I can't go in either." He grimaced. "That sucks."

"Yeah, it sure does." Kady turned towards Todd and crouched on her knees so she could look up at his freckled face. "But I bet you get to do lots of other fun things in camp."

He thought for a moment. "We play baseball and dodgeball and stuff like that, but I still like swimming the best. I passed my deep-water test so I can go out real far."

"Well, you're going to have to wait until they catch that bad fish, Todd. The lake's too dangerous right now."

"Yeah, I don't wanna fight with a bad fish. I don't swim *that* good." He glanced at the deceptively tranquil clear water.

The Gonzalez's phone rang shortly after ten o'clock Wednesday morning. "Hello," a deep male voice said. "Can I please speak to Mr. or Mrs. Gonzalez?"

"Who's calling?" Kady asked.

"My name's Doctor Frank Margolies and I'm a marine biologist with Connecticut State Labs...Is this Katy Gonzalez?"

"Kady with a 'd,'" she said automatically.

"Hi, Kady," Dr. Margolies said. "I'm working on identifying the jumping fish you saw in the lake. Is your mother or father available? I'd like to check if it would it be okay if I came over and had you look at some pictures of fish."

"Oh." She paused.

The man seemed to understand the reason for her hesitation. "Listen, I don't have to come into your house," he said quickly. "I could meet you outside."

"I guess that would be okay," the girl said, knowing her father wouldn't like the idea of a strange man coming to the cottage to talk to her. But they would be in the yard, not inside the house. Besides, identifying a dangerous fish sounded much more important and interesting than anything she had planned for the morning. "When will you be here?"

"Just give me thirty minutes." After confirming her address, Dr. Margolies hung up.

Kady was sitting on her front lawn, the notebook of rejected poems next to her, when she heard a car stop nearby. She rose and started walking towards the street.

A balding heavyset man in his mid-forties stood on the front lawn, smiling at her. "Hi, Kady, I'm Frank Margolies," he said, holding out his left hand. In the other, he carried a laptop.

She shook the outstretched hand. "Hi, Doctor Margolies."

"Just call me Frank. It's easier. Let's sit right here to do this." The scientist plopped his hefty body onto the grass, opened the laptop, and turned it on. "We got a heads-up on the autopsy that Martin Urloch was indeed killed by numerous bites and cuts inflicted by some kind of fish," he said, looking up at Kady. "But it's not clear which species it was. We've never had anything like this happen in Peachwood Lake before."

"I know," the girl said. "I never saw a fish jump so high out of the water. Does that happen a lot?"

"Well, there is a fish in a river in Florida that jumps during the summer. It's called a gulf sturgeon—a long silver fish like the one you described—but it doesn't have any teeth, just sharp bony plates...Do you think you could have mistaken bony plates for teeth?"

"No," Kady said, shaking her head adamantly. "The fish I saw had lots and lots of sharp teeth."

"This sturgeon can grow very big—up to eight feet long and weigh as much as two hundred pounds. Was the fish you saw that large?"

"No. It was big. But I'm pretty sure it was only about four feet."

"Let me show you a picture of this gulf sturgeon, just to be sure it's not the one you saw." Frank turned on the computer, opened a photo file, and rotated the screen so it faced the girl. "This fish has injured people, some seriously," he said. "When it jumps, it sometimes hits boaters and, because it's so large and bony, it can hit very hard and hurt them, even knock them into the water."

"Wow!" Kady let out a deep breath. "That's a mean-looking fish.

Do you think it wants to hurt people?"

The marine biologist smiled at her. "Scientists don't consider this sturgeon to be a mean fish at all. It only looks that way. Is it anything like the fish you saw?"

"Well it has the pieces of silver that look like armor. But nothing else is the same. Sorry."

"Let's try some other species." He began fiddling with the keyboard.

"Has anyone else seen the jumping fish in Peachwood Lake?" Kady asked.

"Yes, I think several other people have seen it, probably because some folks have spent lots of time staring at the water since the accident. But the reports haven't been very helpful. The fish appears in the middle of the lake, so when it jumps no one's close enough to get a good look." Frank turned to the girl. "I think you're the only one who's seen the fish more than once, nearer to the shore, and for a longer period of time."

Once again, he moved the computer screen towards her. "Any of these look familiar?"

She saw four rows, each with pictures of five fish. They were all silver and had some teeth. But none looked anything like the jumping fish she had seen.

"No." Kady shook her head. "The fish I saw had a longer body than any of these. And, like I said, it looked like it was wearing armor, and had lots of big sharp teeth."

"Sounds like it could be some kind of barracuda," Frank muttered. "They have a bad reputation as killers, even though they rarely attack people and I've never heard of them jumping out of the water either. They're tropical, so they don't live in the northeast or in lakes like this, for that matter. But I'll show you a picture of a barracuda, just in case."

He typed briefly on the keyboard and faced the laptop towards the girl. The photo on the screen revealed an ominous-looking elongated silver fish with a pointy face and a lower jutting jaw containing many little fang-like teeth.

"That's still not the fish I saw," she said. "The one I saw wasn't as long and its skin wasn't smooth. It had much bigger teeth and its whole mouth was the same size, not like this one."

"Oh boy." The scientist scratched his nearly bald head. "This is quite a mysterious fish. Let me find some others." He showed Kady about twenty additional photos and pictures of long silver fish with sharp teeth. None, however, resembled the fish she had seen.

"Back to the drawing board," Frank said, turning off his computer. "Listen, if you think of anything else—or see the fish again and notice something new—please give me a call." He stood up, reached into his wallet, took out a business card, and handed it to the girl. "Here. Thanks so much for your help."

"But I didn't help," she said.

"Sure you did." He patted her hand lightly. "You helped to narrow down what kind of a fish it isn't, which gets us that much closer to finding out what our mystery fish really is." Then, waving goodbye, the marine biologist walked to his car, waddling slightly.

Kady stared at Frank's card and wondered if she should get a file box. She seemed to have started a business card collection.

CHAPTER 4

Late Wednesday morning, Stan Feinman paced back and forth in his small office, running his fingers through the few strands of graying hair that remained on the edges of his head. He removed his reading glasses, placing them carefully on the desk, and wiped his perspiring forehead with a tissue.

What now? he thought. *How can I save the season?*

Feinman was the owner and director of Fairview Day Camp on Peachwood Lake. He had bought the camp eight years ago from an elderly couple who wanted to retire after having operated the facility for nearly thirty years. Until now, Feinman had no regrets about his purchase. As the only camp permitted on pristine Peachwood Lake, Fairview was filled to capacity each summer and boasted a lengthy waiting list.

And Feinman had made numerous improvements to update the camp: a sand-filled beach play area for the youngest kids; new bathroom facilities—the parents loved that; and a remodeled rec room, with four wide-screen TVs that entertained the kids on rainy days. Several months ago, he had purchased the vacant lot across the street, intending to expand Fairview, nearly doubling its size. The town's planning board had just begun reviewing his site plan and the early word was very positive.

But all this was irrelevant without Peachwood Lake. That's what attracted customers to the camp. He already had to keep the kids out of the water and now the town was threatening to officially close the lake. This morning he'd started getting phone calls from parents asking if he was going to reduce the rates because of the "problems" with Peachwood Lake. A few even threatened to withdraw their kids from camp; they wanted the fees pro rated. It was only the middle of July! The situation was building into a catastrophe.

"That damn fish!" Feinman muttered. He picked up a pencil, broke it in half, and threw it into the wastepaper basket. Then he walked to his chair, sat down, and put his head into his hands. This camp—this "pot of gold"—as he sometimes called it, was supposed to make him and his wife rich when he retired in a couple of years.

Feinman was an assistant principal in an intermediate school in the Bronx, a job he despised. With his pension and the income from the day camp, he and Gloria were planning to retire as wealthy people. They had it all worked out—an around the world cruise, a safari in Kenya, maybe even a pied-à-terre in Manhattan...

"Screw it," he murmured. "I've got to do something." The only eyewitness to what happened in the lake was a thirteen-year-old girl so maybe she was imagining things. *Just a goddamn fish, not a whale.* Suddenly, Feinman had an idea. Looking at his watch, he saw it was 11:30. *Perfect.* He would assemble the kids before lunch and do his demonstration.

—⚐—

Kady sat on her dock working on her latest poem—this one entitled simply, "The Mysterious Fish"—and occasionally staring at the lake to see if any creature in it was jumping. Looking up, she glanced at the water and saw only sparkling blue-green liquid. *Maybe it's gone,* she thought, returning to her work. *Let's see...*The girl began scribbling furiously.

Oh jumping fish of the gleaming lake.
You give us nightmares with your gigantic teeth
that bite so hard.
Why do you want to hurt us?

"More garbage," Kady mumbled, shaking her head as she reread the lines. "No, no, no!" She took her pencil and crossed out everything she had just written.

—⟋⟍—

At quarter to twelve, the entire population of Fairview Day Camp stood on the shore of Peachwood Lake, listening to owner/director Stan Feinman, who faced them with his back against the water. The campers and their counselors squinted and fidgeted. It was uncomfortably hot and they were hungry, anxious to get out of the sun and into the air-conditioned lunchroom. Several counselors stole surreptitious glances at their watches; many kids kicked softly at the sand.

"...I know everyone misses being able to use the lake," Feinman was saying. "It's a shame that the fear of one little fish is keeping you all out of this beautiful water." He paused, sighing theatrically. "I don't think it's necessary to take such drastic action."

Feinman turned around and pointed to the lake. "We already have a rope limiting our swimming area," he continued. "I want to move the rope in several feet for additional safety. That jumping fish has only hurt someone who was in deep water in the middle of the lake. There's absolutely no danger here, right by the shore."

He turned so he again faced his squirming audience, unbuckled his sandals and took off his shirt and shorts, revealing blue-and-white-striped bathing trunks. "Now I'm going to show you all just how safe the lake is." Feinman walked to the edge of the water and quickly stepped in. "This is great!" he shouted. Then, lying on his back, he floated towards the middle of the camp's swimming area.

"Tell your parents this is as far as you'll be allowed into the lake," he yelled as he stood up, the water reaching the middle of his flat stomach. "It's only about three and a half feet." Feinman placed his hand next to his waistline to illustrate the water's height. "Very shallow. We'll give out permission slips this afternoon and, if your parents sign, you'll be able to go back into the water tomorrow. We'll move the markers in to this point." He indicated the floating three-sided chain, which consisted of rope interlaced with red, blue, and yellow balls. "Won't that be great?"

The response to the camp director's question was a smattering of unenthusiastic applause and a few low murmurs of "yay." His audience was more interested in escaping the hot sun.

"Now I'm going for a short swim and then we'll all head for lunch," Feinman said as he turned, dove, and, with a crisp crawl stroke, began swimming towards the deeper water.

—⚭—

Looking up from her notebook, Kady noticed that the entire population of Fairview Day Camp seemed to be standing on the beach. She stood and stared at the scene on the opposite side of the lake. *What's that all about?* she wondered.

Her stomach made a rumbling noise and she glanced at her watch. It was nearly noon. *Time for lunch.* Clutching her notebook, she dashed into the cottage.

Kady took a can of tuna fish from the cabinet and grabbed two slices of whole wheat bread. She mixed the tuna with two tablespoons of mayo and spread it on the bread. Then she poured a glass of milk and sat down to eat. After taking one bite of the sandwich, she put it down. *Mamee*, she thought.

Kady always associated tuna salad sandwiches with her grandmother, who had loved making them for her. She missed Mamee so much. The girl sighed and tried not to think of the sad times, which had begun when her grandmother got sick.

Her dad's mother had lived with them in their Peachwood Lake cottage, helping to raise Kady. But Mamee had gotten cancer. Her dad had taken time off work to care for his mother and that move eventually cost him his job. After Mamee died two years ago, her father had gone into a prolonged funk. He lay on the couch or in bed, sleeping most of the time, drinking a lot of beer, and not doing much else.

Kady had phoned her father's brother, Uncle Victor, who lived in California, hoping he would be able to help. But the two brothers weren't very close and Uncle Victor, who had flown home immediately after Mamee's funeral, offered only sympathy. "Sorry, Kady, I can't come to Connecticut again so soon," he had said. "I just don't have the money right now. Edgar loved Ma so much that he must be really hurting. I hope he'll snap out of it soon."

Her father had no other immediate relatives and no close friends for Kady to turn to either; he had withdrawn from everyone during her grandmother's illness. So she had continued going to school and tried to do the necessary cooking and cleaning.

After about a month, their landlord, a friendly widow named Mrs. Brancusi, had unexpectedly appeared at the cottage early one evening. When the girl had opened the door, the well-dressed white-haired woman had expressed concern about Kady and her father, explaining she had phoned, leaving several messages that Edgar hadn't returned.

"What's going on here?" Mrs. Brancusi had asked. Kady had said nothing and didn't invite the landlord into the house. But the woman had peeked inside and noticed Edgar sleeping on the living room couch with several empty beer cans on the floor.

"So that's why he didn't pay the rent," she had mumbled. Then Mrs. Brancusi hugged Kady, who had begun sobbing, and walked the distraught girl into the kitchen. She had made hot chocolate for both of them and listened as Kady recounted the full story of her grandmother's illness and her father's decline.

"Okay, here's what we're going to do," the woman had said. First she made an appointment for Kady's dad to see a doctor early the next day. Then she woke Edgar and told him her plan. "If you don't come with me to the doctor tomorrow, I'm calling Child Protective Services and you'll lose your daughter," she had threatened.

Edgar had gone to the doctor with Mrs. Brancusi, taken the pills the physician had prescribed, and immediately stopped drinking. He apologized to Kady for his behavior, blaming it on depression. "This will never happen again," he had vowed. And her father had kept his promise. He had found a new job at CompuTechno Industries and was saving money again.

Now Kady and her dad were a small, but happy, family of two. She looked at the tuna sandwich and again thought of Mamee and the good times, remembering her grandmother's laughter and silly Spanish songs. Smiling softly, the girl picked up her sandwich and began eating again.

—‑‑‑

One little girl with pigtails, standing on the beach of Fairview Day Camp, saw it first. "Look!" she shouted. "The jumping fish!"

Campers and counselors quickly turned to see where the girl was pointing. Instead of a jumping fish, they saw a heavy ripple in the water, about twenty feet behind where Stan Feinman swam.

"Get out!" a male counselor yelled, running towards the water.

"Hurry!" a pudgy teenager screamed. She jumped up and down, as if her action would somehow propel the swimmer.

But Stan Feinman, reveling in the cool clear water, was too far away to hear any of the warnings. He continued swimming briskly along the outer limits of the camp's roped-off area.

Most of the counselors and campers stood on the shore, transfixed by the unfolding scene. Two teen male counselors had stepped into the lake and were tentatively walking—not swimming—towards the camp owner, shouting his name.

The long silver fish jumped again. This time, several campers and counselors saw it and pointed animatedly to its location. Now the fish was only a few feet from the camp owner.

Feinman also heard the second splash. "Wha...?" he mumbled, spinning around. As he did, a ferocious-looking fish with a mouth full of razor-sharp teeth jumped at him, latching onto his neck.

"Ow!" Feinman screamed, trying to pry the clinging creature from his body. But the fish held on tightly, biting harder through his skin. Feinman could feel his blood spurting out from a gaping wound that was becoming larger with each bite. "Help!" he tried to shout. But he was already weak from the rapid loss of blood and his voice sounded like a raspy whisper. He sank into the water, now tinged a reddish brown, still trying to break free of the tenacious fish.

—⁂—

Since the weather was very hot and she wasn't allowed to go in the lake, Kady stayed inside after lunch. Deciding to listen to music, she found her portable CD player and a few recordings by her favorite artists and lay on her stomach on the living room floor. After turning on the music, she closed her eyes.

Ashlee, she thought. She used to listen to that CD with Ashlee. Kady sat up and frowned, wondering what was wrong with her today. *Why'm I thinking about all this sad stuff?* She tilted her head and considered her own unspoken question. *Maybe it's because of Mr. Urloch...*She remembered what he had looked like when they took his body out of the lake. Shaking her head back and forth, she tried to erase the horrible image from her mind.

She missed Ashlee. Kady put her arms around her legs and sighed. Ashlee had been her best friend, really her only friend. The shy, skinny girl had lived just a few blocks away and the two of them hung out together all the time—usually listening to CDs and talking about boys. Ashlee's parents didn't have much money either so she and Kady rarely went to the mall, the movies, or other places frequented by the school's popular girls.

But six months ago Ashlee's family had moved to a town in southern New Jersey called Willingboro. At first, the girls had talked on the phone several times a week. They were both lonely and missed each other. However, after about a month, Ashlee made a new friend and the phone calls became more and more infrequent. When they did talk, all Ashlee wanted to chat about was her new best friend, Janine, and how great she was. Kady tried not to be jealous, but it was so hard. Ashlee had a friend and she didn't. It wasn't fair!

Lying on the floor again, Kady closed her eyes, trying to get the memories of Ashlee out of her head. *Just listen to the music*, she told herself.

—m—

On Fairview's shore, campers and counselors first stood in total silence, many with their mouths open, forming expressions of shock and amazement. Then one little boy started screaming. An older girl began sobbing and soon most of the campers and many counselors—the majority just teens themselves—were crying and screaming hysterically.

As quickly as they could, a few of the group leaders herded the shrieking children and stunned counselors into the nearby lunchroom. One counselor had the sense to use her cell phone to call 911 and report what had just happened.

The two young male counselors, still in shallow water, ran out of the lake, too terrified to venture closer to Stan Feinman. Besides, they couldn't see where he was anymore. The camp owner had disappeared into the depths of the once-again calm and clear water of Peachwood Lake.

CHAPTER 5

"Kady! Kady!"

When she heard Todd call her name Wednesday afternoon, Kady was again sitting cross-legged in the middle of her dock trying to revise her "Mysterious Fish" poem.

Her young next-door neighbor ran up to her, completely out of breath. "Did you hear what happened?" he said, panting loudly.

"No. Why are you home from camp so early?" Kady checked her watch; it was only 1:15. She looked up and saw Todd's mother, Jill, walking slowly towards them.

"The fish..." Todd said, still gasping. "It killed Mr. Feinman dead and I saw the whole thing."

"What are you talking about?"

"He wanted to show us that the water was safe, so he went swimming and the fish jumped up and bit him hard...I could see the blood goin' down his neck and everything. All the girls were crying and screaming." Todd stopped talking and waited for her reaction.

Kady just stared at her young neighbor, too shocked to speak.

"What a horrible thing," Jill Cimino said, stepping onto the dock. "And for Todd and all those kids to have to stand there and watch it happen." She shook her head and sighed. "I can't believe that man was foolish enough to swim in the lake after what happened to Martin Urloch."

"He was full of blood, just like in the movies," the boy said. "I could see it all over..."

"Todd, stop it!" his mother ordered. "It wasn't a horror movie. This really happened and now poor Mr. Feinman is dead."

Pouting, Todd lowered his blond head. "It was too like a movie," he muttered.

Jill turned to Kady. "Of course, they closed Fairview," she said. "So now I really need your help. Could you watch Todd weekdays until we can get him into another day camp? I'm going to call camps, but from what I've heard, I think we'll have to wait until August." The woman shrugged. "That's another two and a half weeks, plus the rest of this afternoon. I know this is your summer vacation, but do you think you'd want the job?"

The girl hesitated for just a moment and Jill gave her an anxious look. "Please, Kady. I can't take all those days off. I'll pay you a lot more than what we worked out for after school. I'll make lunch every day and..."

Kady didn't let the woman continue. "Don't worry," she said. "I want the job." Smiling at the boy, she put her arm around his shoulder. "We'll have fun together." She liked Todd and could certainly use the money. Besides, it would give her something better to do than writing bad poems.

"Yeah!" he shouted. "We'll look for the jumping fish and I'll catch it and kill it dead!"

"Todd!" his mother said, scowling at him. "You're not going anywhere near that fish."

"I know...I was just pretending."

"We'll pretend together," Kady said. "C'mon. Let's go to your house." Picking up her notebook, she jumped off the dock, and began walking to the cottage next door. Todd and his mother kept pace alongside her.

—m—

After dinner, Kady and Edgar sat in their living room watching the local news. "We begin tonight with a tragic story," the blond anchorman said. "There's been another death in Peachwood Lake. We're going out to Rachel Castell who's reporting live at the scene."

The picture shifted to an attractive redhead standing at the edge of the lake. "I'm here at Fairview Day Camp, the site of today's terrible water tragedy," the reporter said. "At about noon, Stanley Feinman, the owner of this camp, went into the water to demonstrate how safe it was." She sighed. "But unfortunately, he was very wrong; the water wasn't safe at all and the situation quickly became a terrible nightmare. As this whole camp of young children and teenagers watched and screamed in horror, a jumping fish, apparently the same one that attacked Martin Urloch in his rowboat on Monday, killed Stanley Feinman.

"Mr. Feinman's body drifted to the shore later in the afternoon. Like Martin Urloch, his neck was slashed and he was covered with bite marks." The young woman stopped talking and stared into the camera. "This time there's no doubt. There were hundreds of kids and teens standing right here." Turning around, the reporter spread her arm to indicate where the children had stood. "They all saw a jumping fish with lots of large teeth attack and kill Stanley Feinman. It was a terrible, traumatic experience for all of them." She shook her head sadly.

The TV picture switched to the blond anchorman sitting solemnly behind his studio desk. "Rachel, has the town released the results of the autopsy report on Mr. Urloch?" he asked.

The redheaded reporter's face again appeared on the screen. "Yes, Rob," she said. "But the results weren't very helpful. They confirmed that he was killed by a fish. But they weren't able to determine the species."

"That's what Frank told me," Kady interjected.

"Shh," Edgar said. "Let's listen."

"...related news, Mayor Turnbull has announced that Peachwood

Lake is now officially closed to both swimmers and boaters," the anchorman said. "Tomorrow morning, the police will attempt to capture the fish. We wish them luck." He lowered his head for a moment. "Our next story concerns..."

Edgar switched off the television and glanced at Kady. "Who's Frank?"

"He's the marine biologist I told you about—Doctor Frank Margolies."

"I didn't realize you were on a first name basis...You know I didn't want any more strangers coming to the house."

"He wasn't inside," she murmured.

Edgar continued to stare. "How long was *Frank* here?"

"Only about half an hour...Dad, he told me to call him Frank, so I..."

The phone rang and Edgar, still gazing intently at his daughter, walked into the kitchen and picked up the receiver. "Hello," he said and listened briefly to the caller. "Yes, Kady did mention you. One minute, I'll put her on."

He thrust the phone toward the girl, his hand covering the receiver. "It's for you—your other new friend, Monique. But when you hang up, we're going to finish our talk about how you're supposed to behave with strangers...Okay?"

Kady nodded as she took the phone and Edgar stepped into the living room.

"Hi, Monique," she began. "I guess you're calling because of what happened today."

"You mean that stupid man who got his ass killed swimming in your lake?"

"Yeah."

"*Weird World* updates me about all the latest shit. But that's not why I'm calling. I want to know how you're doing. You were supposed to call me, remember?"

The girl was silent. "Oh," she finally said. "I didn't know you meant it."

"'Course I did. Hey, do you know where I am right now?"

Kady giggled. "How could I know that?"

"Come on. Take a guess."

"Okay...Are you in Hawaii?"

"No such luck, girl. I'm sitting in a cornfield in the middle of the beautiful state of Kansas."

"What're you doing there?"

"Here's what happened. Last night, a Mrs. Candace Tompkins of Ransom, Kansas saw a UFO land in the back of her cornfield. She sat in her kitchen and watched the field until, twenty minutes later, she saw the UFO take off again. Being a devoted reader of our great publication, she called *Weird World* with this breaking news. So now here I am, sitting in my rental car, on the edge of this goddamn cornfield, waiting for a damn flying saucer to land again." Monique laughed loudly. "Yeah, it's a regularly-scheduled UFO, with arrivals every night at eight o'clock at the Tompkins cornfield...Or maybe it'll rotate...One night here, one night at the next-door-neighbor's farm." She giggled. "Sorry, Kady. I think sittin' out here is making me crazy."

The teen chuckled. "You're so funny, Monique. Maybe you should write funny stuff."

"Hey, girl. What'cha think this is? I *do* write funny stuff." The tone of her voice became more serious. "But I really did call to find out how you are doing...So what's goin' on with you?"

"Well, because of what happened to the day camp owner, they closed the camp and now I'm watching Todd, the little kid next door, until his parents find another day camp for him."

"So you got a job. Congratulations."

"Yeah. It'll give me something better to do than write dumb poems."

"There you go again, puttin' yourself down. Gotta stop doin' that, girl."

"I'm sorry, Monique. I'll try."

"Hope so...Listen, I've gotta get off and walk around a bit to see if I missed the UFO fleet. But I want you to call me, even if nothing happens. Just call...Okay?"

"I will." Kady shook her head up and down. "Are you ever coming back here to write a story about Peachwood Lake?"

"Depends on the bosses at *Weird World*. We'll see. Bye."

"Goodbye," Kady said. She hung up the phone and walked into the living room.

Her father turned off the TV and crossed his arms. "As I was saying before, you're going to promise me that you won't talk to strangers anymore. I don't want to find out tomorrow that you made friends with another reporter or scientist or photographer—or any other grownup that you don't know—who happened to come into our yard. Understand?"

"I'm watching Todd so I won't even be here."

"That's besides the point...I don't want you talking to strangers in his backyard either."

Kady nodded her head. "I promise, Dad. Honest."

CHAPTER 6

At nine-thirty Thursday morning, it was already oppressively muggy when four police officers—three men, including Pete Malone, whom Kady had met on Monday, and one woman—paddled to the middle of Peachwood Lake to try to capture the jumping fish. Pete and his partner manned a rowboat; the other two officers operated a small pontoon.

The Peachwood Police Department didn't own any crafts for patrolling the lake so both boats had been borrowed from local residents. Many lake dwellers had offered their vessels since all were eager to reclaim their waterway. Because oil or gas-fueled motorboats were not allowed in the lake, the officers, in case of emergency, had attached a battery-powered trolling motor to the bow of each boat, hoping they wouldn't have to use the portable engines.

The four officers wore life vests and toted an assortment of bait—live fish, mostly minnows, also donated, this time from the local fishing supply store, Peachwood Lake Bait & Tackle—plus chunks of bread and pieces of corn. The police officers carried large hand-held nets and the pontoon—basically a moving float—was equipped with a trawling net attached to its stern. The officers also had Tasers, set very low, which they hoped to use to effectively stun the fish and capture it without damage, enabling scientists to study it and determine its heredity. Although each police officer carried a Glock 9 mm pistol, they felt their everyday weapons wouldn't be very useful in convincing this particular criminal to surrender.

The fish hunters parked their two boats in the middle of the lake about ten feet from each other, began tossing their bait, carefully watched the water, and waited.

—m—

"Look!" Todd shouted as he opened the sliding glass door leading to his patio. "There's people in the lake!" He tossed the box of checkers on the outside table and ran towards the water.

"Wait!" Kady called, racing to catch up to the energetic little boy. She reached the shoreline and stood next to him. "It's the police," she said. "I heard on the news that they'd try to catch the fish this morning."

"Let's watch 'em."

She shook her head. "You've seen enough bad stuff. Let's play checkers like we said we'd do."

"We can play checkers later. I wanna see the cops kill the bad fish dead." The boy attempted to look serious and folded his arms defiantly.

"Todd, we don't know what's going to happen," Kady said, speaking softly. "Maybe someone will get badly hurt like Mr. Urloch or that man from your camp."

The boy frowned at her. "Those guys weren't hurt," he said. "They were killed dead."

"That's what I mean. You shouldn't see any more bad stuff like that."

"Why?" He looked puzzled.

"Because it's not good to see...And you could get nightmares."

"That's what my mommy says. But I never have nightmares." He turned to the girl. "Plea-eeeeeese."

Kady, who was curious too, gave up the fight. "Okay, but just for a little while."

—m—

In the lake, many fish congregated around the police officers' food, eagerly gobbling the minnows as well as the bits of bread and corn. "It's a regular feeding frenzy," the broad-shouldered man on the pontoon shouted to his two colleagues in the rowboat.

"Yeah, but none of them are jumping," Pete yelled back.

"Wait...I think I see something," the woman officer on the pontoon—an attractive brunette in her thirties—said. "Look over there, Scott." She pointed to her right, about fifteen feet away.

Scott turned to the spot she indicated. "I don't see anything. Not even a wave."

"It's gone now. But it was very quick...Keep looking."

Scott used the railing to walk to the side of the rectangular boat. "Diana thinks she saw something move over there," he shouted to the men in the rowboat, pointing to the location.

Pete's partner, an older man with protruding ears, nodded and made an "okay" sign with his right hand. Both officers in the rowboat took out their Tasers.

On the pontoon, Scott craned his head back and forth. "Nothing," he said to Diana.

"It's near us," she replied. "Stay alert." Holding her Taser, she glanced in all directions.

A loud splash erupted at the rear of the pontoon. As Scott and Diana turned towards the sound, they glimpsed a fishtail diving into the water and rushed to the undulating spot where the fish had appeared.

"Did you see it?" Scott called to the men in the rowboat. Pete and his partner nodded and the stocky older officer began rowing closer to the pontoon while Pete held his Taser and net.

Reaching down, Diana lifted the trawling net. "Look," she said. "The fish jumped right through here. It must have bitten a hole in this net."

As Scott knelt to examine the torn mesh, the fish leaped through the opening, hitting him hard in the forehead. The officer fell backwards into the pontoon.

Diana immediately aimed her Taser at the jumping fish. But the creature retreated into the lake and all she hit was splashing water.

"Are you okay?" she asked Scott, who lay sprawled on his back with a bloody gash in the middle of his forehead.

"Yeah," he said, sitting up slowly and exhaling. "That fish packs some punch!"

Diana grabbed the first aid kit and wiped Scott's forehead with a piece of gauze, lifting her eyes constantly to scan the water for the return of the fish. Hurriedly, she applied a band-aid.

"That fish looked like a flying torpedo," the older officer said as he rowed next to the pontoon. "How the hell did it move so fast?"

"I don't know, Harry," Scott said, dabbing the bandage on his forehead. "Let's get the damn thing. Don't take your eyes off the water."

The four police officers sat quietly in their boats, studying the lake for the return of the leaping fish.

"Did you see that?" Todd asked Kady as they sat together in the grass next to Peachwood Lake. "The jumping fish?"

"Yes."

"I think it hit someone. He fell down."

The girl sighed. "I hope he's not hurt too bad. Todd, this is dumb because we can't really see what's going on in the middle of the lake. Besides, it's too hot sitting here in the sun. Let's go back inside and play checkers. Bet I can beat you."

"No. Maybe the fish'll jump again. I wanna see."

"Just a few more minutes," Kady said as she wiped the sweat from her neck and forehead.

The four officers sat in the two boats, eyes focused on the water when suddenly, without warning, the fish jumped again, crashing heavily into Harry's left shoulder. The overweight man lost his balance—the Taser and net falling out of his hands—and he tumbled into the lake, nearly capsizing the rowboat.

"Harry!" Pete shouted as he tried to steady the boat with one hand while waving his net with the other hand in a futile attempt to catch the fish.

Scott and Diana fired their Tasers at the leaping creature, but again hit only water.

Harry surfaced immediately. "I'm fine, Pete," he said. "Don't worry about me. Just get the damn fish!" Holding onto the rowboat, he began hoisting himself up. "Ow! My leg!" he shouted. "F___ing thing's chewing my foot!"

Pete took his net and thrust it into the water, banging the metal shaft against the fish's body. "It's not letting go," he yelled as Harry groaned and shook his leg, trying to free himself from the attached fish. "Damn thing feels like it's made of armor. Can't get a clear shot at it 'cause I'm afraid I'll hit you." Dropping the useless net, Pete reached over to help his hefty partner into the small boat. It was a difficult task; Harry weighed more than two hundred pounds.

On the pontoon, Scott threw off his shoes, dove into the water, and swam to the rowboat.

"Watch out," Pete warned. "It's still got a tight grip on Harry."

"Get him into the boat," Scott said as he lifted Harry by the buttocks and pushed the writhing man into Pete's arms. "It's still a fish. It can't live out of the water."

Harry lay on the floor of the rowboat, gasping and bleeding profusely from a large raggedy wound above his right ankle. The fish was not in the boat.

"Scott, get out of there fast!" Pete yelled. "It's still in the water."

Scott swam quickly to the nearby pontoon and Diana helped him onto the floating boat. "I've already called for medical help," she said as he sat breathing heavily, water pouring from his soaked clothes.

"We're all heading back to shore."

—m—

"The fish hit the cop and he fell into the water!" Todd shouted. "Then the other cop helped him back up. Wow! That was way cool!"

"I hope the policeman wasn't hurt," Kady said. "We can't see what happened to him." She stood and pointed to the two boats. "Look, Todd. The police are using engines to come back fast. I've never seen that in Peachwood Lake."

"Vroom!" the boy raced around her in a circle, doing his imitation of a speedboat.

"Please stop, Todd. It's too hot out here to run around like that. You're getting yourself all sweaty and we can't go swimming. C'mon. Nothing else is going to happen in the lake right now, so let's go inside and play checkers."

"Okay." He stopped running and faced the older girl. "But that was super fun, wasn't it, Kady?"

"No, it wasn't. I didn't see them catch the fish so I think it was just more super bad stuff." The boy began skipping to the cottage while Kady followed slowly behind.

CHAPTER 7

"...Peachwood police officer Harry Conklin is in stable condition tonight at Middleton Hospital with a serious leg wound he received this morning after being bitten by the fish he was trying to capture—the same jumping fish that is already blamed for the deaths of a swimmer and a boater this week on Peachwood Lake," the blond anchorman said. "One of the officers, Pete Malone, repeatedly banged a pole on the fish's head, but the creature wouldn't let go. Officer Malone said the fish's skin felt like it was made of armor." The newscaster sighed theatrically. "Unfortunately, he and the other officers with him failed to kill the fish." He turned to his right before continuing. "We now go to Rachel Castell who is live in front of Peachwood Town Hall. Rachel?"

The TV picture shifted to the pretty redheaded reporter standing in front of a two-story brick building. "Thank you, Rob. I've just come from a brief press conference called by Mayor Turnbull. The mayor told us that she will hold an emergency meeting here tomorrow night to get input from town residents and businesses on their suggestions as to how to get rid of the fish. This is what the mayor said."

The scene switched to the disheveled-looking mayor, sitting solemnly at her desk, holding a sheet of paper. "Good evening," the woman said. "As you all probably know by now, the police have been unable to capture the murderous fish, so we must explore other alternatives in order to reclaim our lovely lake." She tilted her glasses slightly to the left. "We will have an open meeting tomorrow night—Friday—at eight o'clock at Town Hall to consider all our options. I strongly urge all Peachwood residents to attend." The mayor removed her glasses, put down the piece of paper, and stared directly at the camera. "If you want to again be able to swim and boat in Peachwood Lake, please be here tomorrow night."

Edgar turned off the television with the remote and spoke to his daughter. "So now you know what happened to the policeman who fell into the lake today."

"Yeah," Kady said. "At least he wasn't killed. Todd wanted to watch, but we couldn't really see what was going on when the man was in the water."

"Couldn't you and Todd have done something else this morning?"

"Dad!" the girl shouted. "I already told you it was Todd's idea to sit there and watch the boats. I kept trying to get him to go inside."

"I bet you didn't try too hard," Edgar said. "But that's enough about the fish. Let's talk about something else." He hesitated a moment. "How about another game of Scrabble?"

"Dad, can we go to that meeting tomorrow night?"

"It's going to be a zoo. Lots and lots of people and probably nothing will be decided...We can read about it in Saturday's paper or watch TV to find out what happened."

"I'd really like to go. Remember, I was the first one to see the jumping fish."

"The meeting's meant for adults, Kady. You're only..."

"I'm not a child!" she shouted. "I stay home by myself all day. And now I've got a job watching Todd." She walked to her father and knelt at his feet, grasping both of his hands. "Please."

Edgar grimaced. "All right, we'll go. But I still think you'll be disappointed. This kind of meeting's not like in a movie where things get decided." He shook his head. "It's going to be crazy."

"I don't care," Kady said. "I just want to be there."

—m—

As Edgar and Kady prepared to leave their house Friday night, the weather conditions deteriorated. Deafening blasts of thunder shook the cottage, steady flashes of lightning illuminated Peachwood Lake, and a pounding rain pummeled the roof.

"Are you sure you still want to go?" Edgar asked as he opened the living room curtains to get a better view of the downpour.

"It's just rain, Dad, and this meeting's real important." She put on her raincoat, lifted the hood over her head, and stepped outside.

"Ugh," Edgar mumbled. Grabbing his umbrella, he locked the door and cautiously negotiated the five-mile trip to Town Hall in his trusty ten-year-old Civic. It was still raining heavily when he reached the lot and found a parking spot. "It's almost full," he said. "There may not be any seats left inside."

"Then we'll stand," Kady said, opening the door.

"Spoken by someone who's thirteen-years-old and hasn't worked all day."

"Excuse me?" Releasing the door handle, she turned to her father. "You seem to have forgotten that I now have a full-time job. I spent all day today watching a little boy. That's pretty tiring stuff."

"Sorry, Kady," he said, smiling. "But you've still got more energy than me. After all, you are thirteen."

The girl jumped out of the car, slammed the door, and ran into the building. After locking the car, Edgar opened the umbrella, and followed his daughter inside.

As he had correctly surmised, Town Hall was already packed with people. Kady raced into the meeting room, whizzing past several women who were busy closing their umbrellas, and found two seats in the right corner of the last row.

"Over here!" she shouted to her father, waving her arms as he appeared in the doorway.

Placing his dripping umbrella on the floor, Edgar sat next to Kady and glanced at his watch. "We're early," he said. "It's just ten to eight and I think you got the last two seats. I knew this would be crazy tonight."

"Yeah." She nodded her head and grinned. "It's gonna be great." She looked around the room. "Did you see who's here? Mrs. O'Hara is right over there." She pointed to the center of the third row. "And Mr. and Mrs. Winzinski are all the way on the other side." Leaning towards her left, the girl pointed again. "Isn't that Mrs. Becht two rows in front of us?"

Edgar followed Kady's finger. "Yes, it is." Hearing her name, the gray-haired woman turned around, saw the Gonzalezes, and waved. Father and daughter smiled at the woman and returned her wave.

"Look, there's the mayor," Kady said as the middle-aged woman they had seen on TV the last few days took a seat behind a desk in the front of the room. She wore an ill-fitting light blue pantsuit that seemed to accentuate all her unwanted bulges. Four other people—a tall and bearded older man, an attractive brunette in her early thirties, a bald African-American man, and a tiny blonde woman—entered and sat behind desks on both sides of the mayor.

"They're the Town Board members," Edgar whispered to Kady. A white-haired heavy woman holding a recording device entered next and sat to the side of the town officials. In the crowded front right aisle, a young man in torn jeans set up a video recorder on a tripod.

"Let's begin the meeting," Mayor Turnbull said, gazing at the audience. It was 8:05, every seat was filled, and latecomers stood on all sides of the room. "As you know, we have had to close Peachwood Lake because of the threat of a dangerous fish. This mysterious jumping fish—we haven't been able to determine its species—has killed two people, a boater and a swimmer, and yesterday morning it attacked one of our police officers. Luckily, Officer Conklin survived, although he does have a serious leg injury."

The mayor sighed and shook her head. "We were hopeful that we could capture the fish quickly and reopen the lake, but that hasn't happened so now we have to come up with a workable solution...I will open the meeting to suggestions from the audience. Please give your name and address when you speak."

Many people raised their hands. The mayor pointed to a ruddy-faced middle-aged man in the center of the second row.

"I'm John Garritty and I live on Oakridge Street," he said. "Just poison the water. It'll kill all the fish, including the one we want. Then, I'm sure, there's some chemical that can remove the poison."

The audience members fidgeted uncomfortably in their seats and several people booed. "No!" a young woman with long brown hair standing in the back of the room shouted. "That's not a solution! That's murder! Poison and chemicals in the lake water killing all the..."

"Please!" the mayor interrupted. "Wait your turn. We're just taking suggestions now so if you don't like what someone says, raise your hand and offer an alternative."

"Sorry," the young woman said, speaking in a much quieter tone. "It just sounded so awful."

"I'd like some other ideas." Mayor Turnbull scanned the room. "Yes, Mr. Sanchez."

"Thank you, Mayor Turnbull." A short Hispanic man with a thin mustache rose from his first row seat and turned around so he faced the majority of the crowd. "Many of you know me, but for those who don't, my name is Alfredo Sanchez and I own Row Your Boat Rentals. For most of you, not being able to swim or boat in the lake is an unfortunate inconvenience. But for me, it's much more than that. It's my business." He put his hands on his chest for emphasis. "When the lake is closed, I don't make any money. It's the same for Steve Busch who runs Peachwood Lake Bait & Tackle." He pointed to an older man with a white Santa-like beard sitting two seats to his left, who acknowledged Sanchez with a slight wave. "And it's also true for Danny Thompson, the operator of Peachwood Sailing School." A handsome man in his late twenties with curly long blond hair, who was sitting next to Sanchez, rose, bowed slightly to the audience, and then sat again.

"There was another business on Peachwood Lake," Sanchez added. "But, as you all know, Stan Feinman, the owner of Fairview Day Camp, was attacked and killed in the water earlier this week." He lowered his head and stood silently for several seconds. "For our businesses, we need the lake reopened as soon as possible. Our idea is to get professional divers into the water. Of course, they must be protected in some way and carry weapons that can destroy the fish."

People in the audience whispered to each other about the suggestion. "What do you think?" Kady asked her father.

"I don't know," Edgar said. "It could still be very dangerous."

"That's an interesting idea and we will certainly consider it," Mayor Turnbull said, nodding her head. "Anyone else?" She pointed to a heavy bald man standing near the rear door.

"I'm William Poplevich from Lakeview Drive. On what Mr. Sanchez just said, is there any way you could put divers in some kind of protective steel cage, like they do when they hunt sharks?"

"I doubt it," the mayor said. "This is a smaller fish so a cage would have to have very narrow openings. We'll check, but I don't think it's going to be possible."

She gazed around the room for other raised hands and pointed to a middle-aged woman with short curly hair sitting in the center. "Yes?"

"My name's Maddie Heinrich from Concord Road. How about hiring professional fishermen? A large boat and people who know how to catch all kinds of fish."

"That's an excellent idea," Mayor Turnbull said. "But large fishing boats have engines that will pollute the water." She addressed the audience. "Do you want to allow a motorboat in the lake?"

Shouts of "No!," "No way!," and "No oil pollutants!" filled the room.

Kady turned to her father. "The police used motorboats

yesterday."

"I'm sure those boats had portable batteries, not oil," Edgar explained.

The mayor faced Maddie Heinrich. "At this time, the people are against allowing a commercial fishing boat on the lake," she said before turning towards the entire crowd. "However, that situation may change if we are unsuccessful destroying the fish in a more ecologically-friendly way."

Mayor Turnbull paused and surveyed the room. "Some other ideas?" She motioned to a young man with a wispy goatee standing on the left.

"I'm Tom DeNunzio and I live on Oakridge. Do we know for sure it's just one fish?"

People in the crowd again began whispering to each other. "That's a good question," the mayor said. "Anyone care to comment?"

A white-haired woman, sitting in the second row, quickly raised her hand. "Go ahead," Mayor Turnbull said.

"My name is Frances McCallister from Aurora Road. I've lived here all my life and I love to sit out on my deck and relax, looking at the lake. Since all this has happened, I've spent even more time watching the lake, looking for the jumping fish." The woman stood and faced the back of the room. "There is only one fish that jumps. It's usually in the middle of the lake, but it moves around. I've never seen two fish jumping...I'm sure there's only one jumping fish."

The mayor smiled at the elderly woman. "Thank you for your input—and for watching the lake so closely."

She scanned the room. "Are there any other suggestions?"

A tall African-American woman with very short hair raised her hand. "Yes?" the mayor asked.

"Sandra Forsythe and I live on Lakeview Drive. I know this sounds drastic, but is there any way you could empty the water in the lake and scoop out the fish and keep them in some sort of holding tank?"

In the audience, people shook their heads and whispered among themselves. "I don't know if that's possible," Mayor Turnbull said. "Even if it was, the procedure sounds very long, very complicated, very expensive, and..." The mayor noticed a thin stubble-faced man with small wire glasses in the middle of the third row anxiously waving his hand. "You have some information to add?"

"Maybe," he said. "My name's Brad Esposito from Concord Road. "I just wanted to say that if you drain the lake—even if there was some way you could save all the fish—you'll still kill all the plant life under the water and ruin the whole ecological habitat."

The crowd murmured and the mayor nodded in agreement. "Good point."

Edgar turned to his daughter. "Have you heard enough yet?" he whispered. "Are you ready to go home?"

"No!" Kady said, shaking her head vehemently. "It's too important and it's not crazy like you said it would be."

Edgar sighed. "All right, we'll stay. But like I told you, nothing's going to be decided tonight."

Father and daughter sat through two more hours of listening to additional ideas from residents on how to destroy the jumping fish. As it neared midnight, the suggestions and counter-comments became more and more bizarre: bomb the lake ("You're out of your mind!"), add a dye to the water that would color all the fish ("Don't put any chemicals into the lake!"), and play loud music to upset the fish ("That's noise pollution!"). Finally, no more hands were raised and the room became quiet.

"Thank you all for coming and contributing your ideas," Mayor Turnbull said. "The Town Board and I will meet tomorrow to review the suggestions and decide on a course of action. We will make our decision as soon as possible and alert the media, so you'll be able to hear it on radio or TV, see it on the Internet, or read it in the newspaper. By the beginning of next week, we should have a viable plan in place." She smiled softly. "Hopefully, our new plan will work."

CHAPTER 8

Late Saturday morning, Kady made a phone call. "Hi, Monique," she said. "It's Kady. I'm calling like you asked."

"Hey, girl! What's goin' on with you?"

"Nothing much. But the fish in Peachwood Lake hurt a policeman's leg yesterday. Then we had a town meeting last night about how to get rid of it and my dad and I went."

"Sorry about the cop. Did they decide anything at the meeting?"

"No."

Monique chuckled. "They never do. People just talk a lot and make a bunch of suggestions, most of them dumb."

"That's exactly what happened." Kady said. "My dad warned me. But I still wanted to go 'cause it's so important and I saw the fish first. The mayor said she'd meet with the Town Board and they'd do something early next week."

"Let me know what they decide," Monique said, chuckling again. "Think of yourself as a junior reporter."

"Okay. Should I write down all the stuff that happens?"

"Sure. You want to be a writer, so write."

"I'll start doing that now." Kady hesitated briefly. "Hey, Monique, what happened with the flying saucer? Did you ever see anything in that cornfield?"

"What do you think happened?"

"Nothing?"

"You got it. No saucer landed or took off. But the lady insisted it would come back. If it does, I'm not gonna be the one sitting out in that shitty field looking for it."

"So what're you doing now?"

"Well, today I'm off. I'm meeting a couple of friends and we're going to the beach. Then, on Monday, I'm interviewing a man in Staten Island who claims there's a ghost living in his attic."

"That sounds really cool!"

"Nah, it's not," Monique muttered. "You wouldn't believe how many nuts out there see ghosts. We get these jerks calling us every week."

"I'd love to go with you."

"Maybe sometime you'll be able to. But, right now, you've got to keep me up to date on what's going on with your crazy jumping fish."

"Are you coming back here to do a story about Peachwood Lake?"

"Depends on what happens. If they find out the fish's from another planet or some kind of ghost fish, then you better believe I'll be there."

"Oh," Kady said quietly and then she was silent.

"Hey, girl, don't pout. I'll be back anyway to see you."

"Really?"

"Really." Monique spoke rapidly. "Listen, I gotta get ready to meet the guys. But I'll call you soon and you can always call me, just to talk, or if something important happens with your fish. Remember, you're an assistant reporter now."

"Yeah, I remember," Kady said, smiling. "Bye, Monique."

"Bye, Kady girl."

A few minutes after her phone conversation with Monique, Kady grabbed her notebook and pencil, stepped through the sliding glass door, and walked past a new addition to her familiar backyard landscape. Yesterday afternoon, as she and Todd watched, a college kid named Ryan had hammered a six-foot wooden post between their properties. On it, he had nailed a white plastic sign with big black capital letters that read, "NO SWIMMING OR BOATING IN THE LAKE!" The word "NO" was underlined in red. On the bottom right, in much smaller letters, were the words "Town of Peachwood." Ryan told them he and two other college students were erecting the signs all around the lake.

Kady continued walking to the edge of her dock and faced the glistening clear water of Peachwood Lake. From the living room window, Edgar saw the girl standing quietly, just staring at the water. Quickly, he put on his sneakers and headed to the backyard. "What are you doing out here?" he asked as he reached his daughter.

"I'm just looking for the jumping fish," she said. "Maybe I'll notice a pattern or something, like that lady said last night." Turning towards her father, she pointed to her notebook, which lay on the front of the dock. "Monique made me an assistant reporter and I'm supposed to write down stuff that happens with the fish and the lake."

Edgar smiled. "That sounds like a great job for a beginning writer like you. But that woman at the meeting spends hours and hours just staring at the water." He patted Kady's shoulder and gazed at the cloudless, bright blue sky. "You're young. You should be doing other things like girls your age. It's hot and sunny today so why don't we spend the afternoon at Renfrow Park? They've got a pool there so you can swim and, if you bring your notebook, then you can write too."

"What about food shopping?" Kady asked. They usually went to the supermarket on Saturday.

Edgar shook his head. "Too nice a day today. We'll go shopping later tonight or tomorrow. C'mon. Let's go inside and get ready." He put his arm around his daughter's shoulders and together they walked back to the cottage.

—◊—

Kady and Edgar arrived at Renfrow Park in the early afternoon and discovered they were not alone. "Maybe this wasn't such an great idea," Edgar said as they searched the grassy area surrounding the pool for a place to lie down. Finally, a couple of bikini-clad young women sunning themselves moved over so he and Kady had just enough room to spread their towels.

Father and daughter removed their tee shirts and shorts, revealing their bathing suits. As Edgar applied suntan lotion, Kady reached into their canvas bag for the mystery novel she was reading, plus her pad and pencil. Then she scanned the dense crowd. "I've never seen so many people in this park," she said.

"Me neither," he agreed. "But it makes sense. It's Saturday, it's hot, and with Peachwood Lake closed, this is the only free swimming place in town."

Kady pointed to the pool. "The water's jammed too. People can hardly move."

"At least we'll be able to cool off," Edgar said. "Here. Put some lotion on." He handed the tube to her. "I'll do your back and then you can do mine." After both of them were fully lotioned, the girl lay on her stomach and read her mystery novel while her father closed his eyes.

A few minutes later, Kady sat up and tossed the book on the grass. "Dad, it's much too hot just lying here," she said. "I'm going in the water."

"Go ahead and cool off," Edgar said, keeping his eyes closed. "I'm okay so I'll stay here and watch our stuff."

She picked up her towel and walked to the pool.

—◊—

When Kady stepped into the water, the pool was still crowded. Several little kids shouted and splashed noisily in the shallow end while groups of adults stood along the sides of the deeper section, submerged to their necks, many chatting with the people next to them. One teen couple in the corner groped each other and kissed. Noticing the pair, Kady immediately glanced away.

"Look! It's Fraidy Kady!"

The girl heard her name and cringed, knowing the taunting voice belonged to Hannah Evans. In fifth grade, Kady had been frightened by a spider in the school bathroom and had let out a shriek. Unfortunately, of all her classmates, Hannah had been the one to hear it. Now Kady turned around and saw the blonde-ponytailed girl swimming towards her while three of Hannah's friends—part of her clique—crouched in the water nearby, watching and smiling.

"What're you doing here?" Hannah sneered. "You always stay at *the lake*." She pronounced the last two words with total disgust.

"I guess you didn't hear that Peachwood Lake is closed," Kady said, trying to imitate Hannah's haughty tone. "This is a town pool so it's open to everyone."

"Yeah, well you're not everyone," Hannah said, pausing for dramatic effect. "You're *no one*." Then, turning her back on Kady, she swam towards her friends.

Even with all the noise in the pool, Kady could hear the four girls laughing loudly. She stifled her tears, trying to block out the painful words, and didn't immediately run out of the pool, knowing if she did, the girls would laugh even harder. After forcing herself to stay in the water for several long minutes, she rushed out of the pool, grabbing her towel.

"Bye, Fraidy Kady!" she heard Hannah shout. "Go back to your stupid lake!" Hannah and her friends giggled as they swam away.

This time, Kady couldn't stop the tears. They streamed down her face as she ran towards her father.

—◊—

Edgar, his eyes still closed, heard Kady spread her towel on the grass. "How was the water?" he asked. When she didn't answer, he opened his eyes, looked at his daughter, and realized she had been crying. "What happened?" he asked, sitting up.

"Hannah and her friends were in the water and she was mean to me again," Kady said, her eyes starting to tear once more.

"Oh crap." Edgar reached over to hug his daughter. "I don't know what's wrong with that stupid girl. Maybe I should call her mother."

'No!" Kady shouted, pulling away from her father's grasp. "That'd make it even worse! She'd just call me more names." Then she spoke quietly. "I just want to stay far away from her."

Edgar shook his head. "We'll try."

Kady tried to read her mystery novel, but although the book was engrossing, she couldn't concentrate. She kept hearing Hannah's taunting sing-song voice repeating, "Fraidy Kady! Fraidy Kady!" Picking up her notebook and pencil, she began writing a short story, titling it "Mean Girls."

> *Anna was very pretty. She was the most*
> *popular girl in school. Anna had a group of friends*
> *who followed her around like little puppies, trying*
> *to copy everything she did. And most of what Anna*
> *did was mean and nasty.*
>
> *Kathy was a quiet girl. She didn't have any*
> *friends. Kathy sat by herself most of the time,*
> *reading or studying. Every time Anna saw Kathy,*
> *she would say or do something to make her sad...*

Kady spent the rest of the afternoon writing her story; she didn't venture back into the pool.

CHAPTER 9

"See, I told you it'd be fun drivin' around tonight," Tiffany Terrizini said to Kevin Hurley as she took another deep slug of beer.

"Yeah, sure," Kevin mumbled. *What does she care?* he thought. She wasn't paying for the gas and she wasn't saving money for college either, unlike Kevin who was going to the University of Michigan in the fall. He stole a quick glance at his date. "Jeez!" he muttered softly. "Tiffany, how many beers have you had?"

She twirled the beer she was holding, glanced down at the discarded bottles under her seat, and giggled. "I dunno, Kev. Three, maybe four."

Kevin winced. He hated the nickname "Kev" and had asked Tiffany several times not to use it. "Maybe you should stop drinking," he suggested.

"Why? It's a real hot night." She giggled again, lifted her blouse, and waved it back and forth to fan herself.

Kevin shook his head, wondering why he had worked so hard to get her to go out with him. But, of course, he knew the answer: Tiffany was super beautiful. She had long and wavy jet-black hair with a bright orange streak, pouty full lips, and a figure that Hollywood movie stars would kill for. He had pursued Tiffany for weeks—texting and IMing her with romantic messages, even sending her gifts of chocolates and flowers—and his efforts had paid off. This was already their third date. But Kevin was losing interest. He sighed. In addition to drinking too much, Tiffany had turned out to be stupid and boring. However, there was one major upside: She was a great lay.

Kevin's conscience was starting to bother him a little. Was he just using her? *Probably*, he thought. But she loved sex, so she was using him too. And look at all this extra driving he was doing just for her. Besides, what would his friends say if he dumped Tiffany? They were already jealous that he had landed the hottest girl in school and would never understand his reasons. They would laugh at him for sure.

Earlier that Saturday evening, he had driven twenty-five miles so Tiffany could see a new slasher movie. "Please, Kev!" she had begged. "It's supposed to be super gory with lots and lots of blood."

It had been super all right—super dumb, with no plot, just axes hacking people up. Naturally, Tiffany had loved it, screaming with delight as the crazed killer chopped off each body part. Kevin had fidgeted in his seat, checking his watch every few minutes, hopeful the stupid film would end.

Finally, all the bodies had been hacked, and now here they were, driving aimlessly around some shitty lake in some shitty town at one in the morning because Tiffany had decided it was a good idea. But his date didn't have any original ideas. *Must've seen characters do this on TV or in a movie.*

"Kev, stop here!" Tiffany ordered, interrupting his thoughts. He stepped on the brakes and gave her a questioning look. "I have to pee," she explained.

He saw an empty parking lot on his left, adjoining the lake, and guided the car into it. "Where are we?" he asked.

"I dunno," Tiffany said, opening the door and running towards the water.

Kevin followed slowly, still trying to figure out their location.

He noticed a large one-story building on his right and a stretch of gleaming sand leading up to the lake. The night was nearly totally dark, with many stars, but very little moonlight. Kevin carried a small flashlight on his key ring. Switching it on, he saw lettering on the front of the building facing the street that read "FAIRVIEW DAY CAMP."

He rushed to Tiffany, who had taken off her sandals and was pulling down her shorts and panties, preparing to squat in the lake. "It's a day camp," he announced.

"So what? Who the hell cares? It's night now and no one's here." Tiffany half-sat above the shallow water and urinated. "Ahh! Much better." She stood up, naked from the waist down, and smiled seductively at Kevin.

"We're all alone," she said, slipping her blouse over her head. "So romantic," she cooed as she unsnapped her bra, wriggling until it fell softly onto the sand.

Although it was very dark, Kevin saw enough of Tiffany's curvaceous naked body to make him want her. *Must've seen a movie about sex on the beach*, he thought as he quickly threw off his clothes.

Tiffany lay down spread-eagle like she was making a snow angel in the sand. Within seconds, Kevin climbed on top of her and it was over very quickly. He gasped and groaned with pleasure while Tiffany, never one to be subtle, shrieked in delight.

Kevin rolled onto his back and gazed at the black, star-filled sky. "I hope no one heard that," he whispered.

The girl ignored his words. "I've always wanted to screw in the sand," she said, sitting up. "It was great, but now I'm all sticky. They never show this yucky part in the movies." She stood and walked, somewhat unsteadily, to the lake.

As Kevin followed her, he noticed a pole near them. "There's a sign here," he said. "Wait a second. I want to read what it says." Not listening to him, Tiffany stepped into the water.

He found his key chain, turned on the mini-flashlight, and read the sign. "Tiffany, get out of the lake!" he yelled. "The sign says 'NO

SWIMMING.'"

"Kev, the water's wonderful—so cool and clean," she said, again ignoring him. "You should come in."

He ran to the edge of the shore. "Tiffany, come out!" he ordered. "The sign says, 'Town of Peachwood.' This is Peachwood Lake. It was on TV. There's a fish in this lake that's been killing people. That's why the sign's here, because this water's dangerous."

"You're such a wimp!" Tiffany shook her head as she dog paddled. "Scared of a stupid little fish." She spoke in a sing-song taunting tone. "I'm goin' for a nice swim—with or without you."

"Don't go in the deep water!" Kevin shouted. But, of course, his date didn't listen. "What's the use?" he muttered. "She's just going to do what she wants anyway." Quickly, he found his clothes and got dressed. Then he sat at the edge of the sand and waited for Tiffany to finish her swim.

—ɯ—

It was quiet except for the little swimming noises Tiffany was making in the water. Then Kevin heard a new sound—a sudden loud splash. He stood, staring at the lake, but it was too dark to see anything. He switched on the little flashlight and held it up. *Nothing.* A few seconds later, he heard the splashing noise again. Moving the light, he caught a brief glimpse of something silver jumping into the water—just a few yards behind Tiffany.

"Swim back here now!" he screamed as loud as he could. "I see the jumping fish! It's right behind you!"

Hearing the fear in Kevin's voice, this time Tiffany listened, immediately swimming rapidly towards the shore. But the fish was much faster. The girl felt a sharp pain as it bit her naked chest and latched onto her body. "Oh my God!" she screamed, trying to yank the tenacious creature off her. The fish, however, seemed to have enormous suction power, chewing deeper into her chest with its many jagged teeth as she wrestled to release its grip.

"Kevin! Help!" Tiffany screamed, just before she was forced

underwater by the relentless fish.

Throwing off his shoes, Kevin rushed into the water, still wearing his clothes. But without hearing or seeing Tiffany, he had only a vague idea of where she was. "Tiffany, I'm coming!" he shouted, moving the flashlight in a 180-degree radius around the lake to try to spot her. "There!" he muttered, seeing her hand raised as she resurfaced for a moment. She was just twenty feet to his right.

When he reached her, Tiffany was motionless, face down in the water, her beautiful hair forming a dark halo around her head. Turning her on her back, he held her with one hand, and swam rapidly to the shore.

Kevin dragged the motionless girl out of the water and placed her on his lap, her long hair cascading over her naked torso. "Tiffany?" he asked. No answer. He felt something oozing down his wet pants. *Blood?* Kevin had lost his little flashlight in the lake, so he couldn't see at all. Tracing the source of the flowing liquid with his finger, he found it was coming from a gaping wound in her chest. The blood was leaking out from her heart!

"No...ooo!" He clutched the girl's lifeless body and sat by the edge of the water shrieking hysterically.

All around Peachwood Lake, lights switched on, one by one, and soon the water reflected many sparkling flashes of yellow. But Kevin didn't notice the beauty of the nighttime scene. He continued to hold Tiffany and wail.

CHAPTER 10

The whirring sound of an emergency vehicle's siren woke Kady. Wondering if it was because of the fish, she quickly checked the clock and saw it was very late, about 1:30. Rubbing her eyes, she turned on the light and walked to the window, separating the lacy curtains so she could look at the lake.

Although it was the middle of the night, she saw many lights on in homes that flanked the water, especially those houses on the opposite shore. At the day camp, Kady could make out the forms of several autos, including one with spinning red beams that had to be a police car. As she watched, a larger vehicle with flashing lights pulled into the parking lot.

Remembering her new position as assistant reporter for Monique, Kady found her notebook and pencil. Then, after pushing her chair next to the window, she started jotting down her impressions of the scene across the lake.

—◊—

"Did you hear the sirens last night?" Kady asked her father as they ate breakfast Sunday morning.

"No. What time was it?"

"After one." She lowered her cereal spoon and stared at him. "I looked out my window and saw some kind of truck—an ambulance or fire engine—go into the day camp. And a police car was already there." She took a bite of frosted flakes cereal.

"You think someone was dumb enough to go into the water over by Fairview?" Edgar asked as he sipped his coffee.

"Uh huh." The girl nodded. "I stayed up a while writing things down for Monique, like I promised. But I didn't see anything else happen."

"That's right," he said, smiling. "You're a junior reporter now."

Kady pointed to the Sunday edition of the *County Courier* that lay unopened on the kitchen counter. "Would it be in today's paper?" she asked.

"No," her father said. "Not if it happened after midnight. But there'll be a story on TV or on the radio." He took another sip. "It's true what they say about bad news; it really does travel fast."

"I'll check anyway." She stood up, retrieved the newspaper, unfolded it to reveal the front page, and glanced at the headline. "You're right, Dad. Nothing here about last night." Then she turned to the second page. "Wait. There's a story about what the Town Board decided to do about killing the fish. Listen." She began reading:

"TOWN TO SEND DIVERS INTO PEACHWOOD LAKE

"Peachwood Mayor Margaret Turnbull announced that the Town Board has decided to send a team of divers from the county's Water Rescue Unit into Peachwood Lake Monday morning to destroy the mysterious fish that is believed to be responsible for the deaths of two men—Martin Urloch and Stanley Feinman—earlier this week.

"Mayor Turnbull said the Board reached the decision after a lengthy emergency meeting. 'We listened to residents' suggestions Friday night and then we kicked ideas around for five more hours on Saturday,' the mayor said. 'We finally decided that dispatching the divers would be the best option for killing the fish. Of course, they'll be well armed and protected...'"

Kady stopped reading. "What do you think?" she asked.

"I don't know," Edgar said, shrugging. "I hope it'll work." He patted her shoulder gently. "C'mon. Let's get ready to go." After spending Saturday at the park, they were doing their supermarket shopping this morning.

Although it was Sunday, father and daughter had reached a compromise regarding church services; they went on alternate weeks. Edgar wanted to attend services every Sunday. But the experience was painful for Kady. Hannah Evans and some of her friends went to the same church—St. Andrew's—and the girls sat in a back pew together during the service, seemingly having a great time. Although Kady had no proof, and her father insisted she was too sensitive and exaggerated things, she always felt the girls were laughing and pointing at her. Several times she even thought she heard Hannah whispering, "Fraidy Kady."

The Gonzalezes had tried attending the early morning service instead, but neither liked waking up at seven o'clock on Sunday. As a result, six months ago they had worked out their alternating-weeks agreement. And today was the off week for church.

"If we go shopping soon, we'll still have time to do something fun this afternoon," Edgar said. "Hurry up and get dressed."

—⟋m⟍—

As father and daughter began putting the groceries away, Edgar noticed the "Message" button on their phone was flashing and immediately pressed "Play." They heard Monique's lilting voice as she identified herself. "Kady," the message continued. "Please call me on my cell when you get back. It's important. Bye."

The girl gave her father a questioning look.

"It's okay," he said, putting a box of spaghetti in the side cabinet. "I'll finish up here so you can go call her. She said it was important."

"Thanks, Dad," Kady said, smiling. Taking Monique's card, which she now kept in her wallet, she dialed the cell number from the kitchen phone.

"Hey, girl!" Monique said.

"Hi. I'm calling like you asked. You said it was important."

"Do you know what happened last night?"

Kady spoke rapidly. "I heard sirens that woke me up and then I saw a bunch of cars across the lake at the day camp. I sat by my window for a while and took notes for you. Then I checked the newspaper this morning, but it didn't have any story about last night. Me and my dad just came back from the supermarket and, after we unpacked, we were going to listen to the news. What happened?"

Monique sighed. "Another person was killed in the lake. This dumbass teenage girl decided to go for a midnight swim at the camp and..."

"Didn't she see the sign?" Kady interrupted. "They put signs up everywhere around the lake telling people not to swim."

"Her boyfriend read the sign and he said he begged her not to go into the water. But she wouldn't listen to him." The reporter hesitated briefly. "He also said she was kind of drunk."

"And kind of stupid. Wow!" Kady let out a deep breath. "Did her boyfriend see the fish?"

"Yeah. He saw it jump. Then he yelled to the girl and she tried to swim back fast. But it was too late."

"That is so awful. But that girl sounds really dumb. I mean, with all the stories on TV and in the papers..."

"She wasn't from Peachwood, Kady, and she doesn't sound like the type of girl like you who reads newspapers or watches the news on TV. Her boyfriend had heard about the fish, but she probably hadn't."

"We read that the town's sending divers into the lake tomorrow to try to kill the fish."

"I know. That's why I'm calling."

"You want me to do something?"

"Not exactly," Monique said. "*I'm* going to do something. I'm coming back to Peachwood Lake to write some stories about your evil fish, starting tomorrow morning when the divers try to kill it."

"That's great! But weren't you supposed to interview a man about a ghost tomorrow?"

"Cancelled it. Next week, some other jerk will see a ghost—or Elvis or the Loch Ness monster. I can write that shitty story anytime."

"Oh," Kady said, hesitating briefly. "But you said your paper wasn't interested unless it was some kind of alien fish or ghost fish. Did you find out something new about the fish?"

"No. We still don't know anything more than you do."

"Then how come you're going to write stories about it?...I don't understand."

"The fish killed a girl, Kady—a beautiful young teenage girl. That kind of shit sells papers. Fish kills a couple of old men, no one cares. But a fish that bites through the heart of a hot sixteen-year-old white chick, our readers want to read about monsters like that. *Weird World*'s decided I'm covering this story, full-time, until your fish is caught. I'm making reservations at the nearest motel—you ever hear of Gateway Lodge in Eastbury?—and I'll be in your neighborhood early tonight." She chuckled. "We're goin' to be seeing a lot of each other, girl."

Monique's question gave Kady an idea. "I don't know anything about that motel," she said. "But please don't make any reservations yet. I've got to check something out first. Can I call you back in a couple of minutes?"

"Sure, hon. Just make sure you call back soon though. I'm packing now so I can get my ass out of here."

"Promise I'll call you real fast. Bye."

As soon as she hung up the phone, Kady turned to her father, who was unloading the last of the groceries. "Did you hear all that?"

Edgar put a can of tuna in the cabinet and looked up. "It sounded like some poor girl went swimming in Peachwood Lake last night and was killed by the fish."

"Yeah. Her boyfriend tried to stop her, but she wouldn't listen... Dad, did you hear the part about a motel? Monique's going to be writing about the fish for her newspaper and she has to stay somewhere around here, near the lake."

"What's the name of the motel she mentioned?"

"I don't know. Some place in Eastbury. But I've got a better idea." The girl walked to her father and held his hands. "Dad, please, can she stay here? We've still got Mamee's bed put away in the attic. We can take it down, set it up, and Monique can sleep in my room. There's enough space."

Edgar released her hands and shook his head. "I don't know, Kady. Monique's your friend, but she's an adult and she's only staying in our neighborhood because of her job. She'd probably be much more comfortable living in a motel."

"Can I at least invite her?"

"Then you'll be putting her on the spot. She might not want to upset you by saying 'no.'"

"I really think she'd like to stay here with us—and we're right on the lake. That motel's not even in Peachwood. Plea-eeeese?"

Edgar smiled. "All right, ask her. But listen carefully to what she says and how she says it. If she sounds at all like she doesn't want to stay in our house, tell her it's fine with you if she goes to a motel." He picked up his daughter's chin and stared into her eyes. "Promise?"

"I promise," she said, grinning broadly as she dashed to the phone.

Kady didn't give Monique a chance to speak. Immediately after hearing her friend's "hello," she jumped in with her proposal. "While you're working here, we'd like you to stay with us."

"That's real sweet, Kady. But I have an expense account and the motel's not far from the lake."

"We're a lot closer and we've got an extra bed in my room and I can make space in my dresser for your clothes and everything."

The reporter was quiet for several seconds. "What does your dad think about this idea?" she finally said.

"That's why I wanted to hang up and call you back. I checked with him and he said it was okay with him unless you really didn't want to stay here."

"Kady, if I stay with you, I want to pay your dad. Like I said, I'm getting money from *Weird World* for this."

"I'll tell him." She turned to her father. "Monique says she wants to pay for staying here."

Edgar shook his head. "No way. We're not running a boarding house. If she stays here, it's as our guest."

"My dad says he won't take your..."

Monique interrupted the girl. "I heard what he said. Let me talk to your father, please."

"Here." Kady handed the phone to Edgar. "She wants to speak to you."

"Hello," he said.

"Hi, Mr. Gonzalez. Kady invited me to stay at your house, but when I offered to pay, you refused. Is that true?"

"Yes. You can stay here as a friend; our guests don't pay."

"That's real nice of you. Now here's my deal—and I won't stay in your house unless you accept it. I get to pay for dinner while I'm living with you. Besides money for a hotel, my paper gives me a big food allowance and I want to use it. Do we have a deal?"

"Well..." His voice faded.

"And, as part of the deal, tonight I want to take you and Kady somewhere special...So name a fancy restaurant that you've always wanted to try."

"I heard people at work talk about the great food at La Champagne, but I've never been there," Edgar said quietly.

"Sounds like a good choice," Monique said with a giggle. "Fancy and French."

"And expensive as hell," he added.

"That's always the case with fancy and French."

Edgar chuckled.

"So do we have a deal?"

"Yes, thank you."

"No, Mr. Gonzalez, *thank you.*"

"Monique, please call me Edgar. You're going to be living in our house as our friend."

"Okay, Edgar. I appreciate that. Listen, I'm almost finished packing and I've got a few things to take care of before I leave. I can be at your house at about five o'clock, if that's all right with you."

"It's fine."

"I'll see you then and don't forget to make reservations for tonight at that fancy French restaurant."

"Yes, I'll do that right now. Goodbye." He turned to Kady, who was grinning broadly, jumping up and down, and clapping her hands. "Okay, we've got a guest coming," he said, smiling at his daughter. "So now we know what we're doing this afternoon. Let's get out the bed and then you go clean your room." He glanced around the kitchen. "I'll work on straightening out the rest of the house. We don't want our guest to feel that she made the wrong choice."

—ɯ—

Monique rang the Gonzalez's doorbell at quarter past five and entered the house wheeling two large suitcases, carrying a smaller duffle bag around one shoulder, and her oversized leather pocketbook on the other. After hugging Kady, she extended her hand to Edgar. "Nice to meet you and thanks again for letting me stay with you."

He took Monique's hand. "You're very welcome," he said,

staring at the array of baggage.

The reporter giggled. "No, I'm not moving in permanently. I just like to be prepared. It's tough when I go on a plane for work and have to cram everything into my carry-on. For here I figured, no luggage fees, no weight limit, no baggage claim—what the heck, I can take anything I want."

Father and daughter helped her stow the luggage in the corner of Kady's room. "Now when's our reservation for?" Monique asked.

"Seven," Edgar said, pushing one suitcase against the wall. "I thought that would give you enough time to unpack and relax a bit. The restaurant's only ten minutes from here."

"Sounds good," Monique said, nodding at him. Then she turned to Kady. "Come on, girl. Keep me company when I unpack."

—m—

Kady, Edgar, and Monique arrived at La Champagne ten minutes early. Each had dressed for the occasion: Kady wore a red and white polka-dot dress with a short flouncy skirt, Edgar had on a navy sport jacket and his best gray slacks, and Monique wore a silky cream-colored dress that contrasted dramatically with her dark-brown skin. After waiting for fifteen minutes, they were escorted to a table in a recessed corner of the small restaurant.

"It's real dark here," Kady said. "Is this the way you eat in a fancy restaurant?"

"Not always," Monique said. "They just put us in a dark corner. Do you want me to ask for another table?" The restaurant was barely half-filled.

"No, that's okay," Edgar said, pointing to the small candle on their table. "There's enough light so we can see our food." He smiled. "This fancy French food will be different and I want to know what I'm eating."

"All right then," Monique said, smiling at Kady and Edgar. "I don't know about you two, but I'm starving since we purposely didn't eat anything at your house before coming here. Let's see if we can get the waiter's attention." They glanced around the room, but didn't notice any servers.

"I'm thirsty," Kady said. "Do you think we can get some water?"

"We should be able to," Edgar said, turning to Monique. "Shouldn't someone come to our table and ask us if we want something to drink?"

"Yeah. That should happen immediately. But, even for a pricey restaurant, this place seems real slow. Let's keep looking for a waiter."

Five minutes later, a waiter headed for a nearby table carrying a small basket of bread. "Excuse me," Monique called, waving her arm. "Can we please have some water? Bread would be good too." She glanced at his basket.

The man, dressed in a shiny black uniform, sauntered to their table. "*Oui, Mademoiselle,*" he said, addressing Monique. "I will inform your waiter." After nodding, he left, taking the basket of bread with him.

After five more minutes, another waiter, younger than the first, ambled to their table. "Good evening," he said, speaking with a thick French accent. "Welcome to La Champagne." He smiled, revealing a mouthful of crooked yellow teeth. "I understand you are thirsty. May I recommend a fine Cabernet Merlot? The Angelus St. Emilion 2005 *c'est extraordinaire.*" He handed both Edgar and Monique a leather-bound wine list.

"Would you like a glass of wine with dinner?" Monique asked Edgar.

"No thanks." He closed the leaflet and gave it back to the waiter.

"You're sure? Don't worry about the price."

"Really...I don't drink alcohol. I'd just like a glass of water."

Monique held the wine list for the waiter. "We'll all have water, please," she said. "With lemon. And a basket of bread."

"Would you like bottled water?"

Monique turned to Edgar, who shook his head. "No," she said. "Tap water's fine."

Without saying a word, the waiter sneered, grabbed the wine list from Monique's hand, and strode towards the kitchen.

"Why's he mad at us?" Kady asked. "What's wrong with regular water?"

"Nothing," Monique said, chuckling. "He just wanted us to spend a lot of money on our drinks, that's all."

Another five minutes later, the waiter returned with three goblets filled with water, no pieces of lemon, and no bread. Without saying a word, he placed the glasses on the table and handed each of them a leather-bound menu. "We'd like some bread," Monique repeated. The waiter nodded and walked away.

They opened the menus. "This is only written in French," Kady said. "I can't read it. Do you know any French, Dad?"

"Only Spanish from listening to my parents and taking it in school." He turned to Monique? "Can you read French?"

"Uh uh." She shook her head. "I figured in New York there'd be more need for Spanish so I don't know any French either. Let's get Silent Sam back to our table and see if he's willing to talk to us." Monique jumped up and waved at the waiter, who stood at the other side of the room, doing nothing. Slowly, he headed towards them.

"*Oui, Mademoiselle,*" he said in a bored tone of voice.

"We can't read the menu because it's all in French. Please tell us some of the dishes you recommend."

He glowered at her. "*La Champagne c'est un restaurant par excellence.* I recommend everything."

Monique glared back at him. "I'm sure you do. But if a customer asks for a suggestion, what do you say?"

"I say, 'Read the menu.' All the food *c'est magnifique.*" He lifted his head and turned up his nose.

Slamming her menu shut, Monique jumped up. "And you know what I say, you dumbass snob? I say, 'You can take your menu and shove it!'" She glanced at Kady and Edgar. "People, we're gettin' outta here. Let's eat dinner at a place that serves good food and knows how to treat its customers." The three of them tossed their linen napkins on the cushioned chairs and marched out of the restaurant.

They ate dinner at a nearby modest café. The food—and the service—were excellent.

—⟫⟫—

As Monique and Kady prepared for bed Sunday night, the reporter took out her laptop. "You've got Internet, right?" she asked.

"Wrong."

"No shit?"

The girl frowned. "Does that mean you can't stay with us?"

Monique was silent for a moment. "You got a library here?"

"Yes. It's on Main Street."

"How far is that?"

"Just a few minutes, near where my dad works." Kady looked puzzled. "How does the library help?"

"I can go there to get an Internet feed when I write my stories so I can email them."

Kady shook her head. "I still don't get it. Why do you need the Internet and email to write your articles? The name of your paper is *Weird World Weekly*. If it comes out weekly, you've got lots of time to write your stuff."

Monique sat on her bed and chuckled. "Girl, *Weird World* may be a weekly, but this is the twenty-first century. We're online too. *Everything* I write goes on our website. We've got plenty of subscribers that want to read this shit online—as soon as it happens—so I gotta write fast and often."

"Wow," Kady said in amazement, lying down in bed. "I didn't know that. So you're a reporter for a weekly, but you still have to write articles daily..."

"And sometimes even more than once a day."

"I'm gonna need a computer to be a writer, aren't I?"

"Yup." Monique nodded.

"Getting the money's going to be tough."

"Just keep saving. You've got plenty of time." She leaned over to Kady and kissed her on the cheek. "Now I want you to be my junior reporter again. I need you to tell me everything you know that happened with the fish, okay?" Monique lay on her stomach, elbows propped up, resting a notepad and a pen on the pillow. "Go ahead."

"Okay...It all started last Monday morning when I was sitting on the dock, writing, and I heard the fish jump..." With as much detail as she could, Kady recounted her experiences watching the fish, seeing the divers retrieve Martin Urloch's body, getting the phone call from the *County Courier* reporter, talking to Dr. Frank Margolies, attending the town meeting, hearing the siren, and observing the late night activity at the day camp.

Monique listened quietly without interrupting and took occasional notes. "Well done," she said when the girl finished. "You've given me lots of background information that I wouldn't have gotten anywhere else. You'll be a terrific reporter...But we've both got real busy days tomorrow, so right now, it's time to go to sleep."

CHAPTER 11

After eating breakfast together Monday morning, Kady, Edgar, and Monique went their separate ways: Kady walked next door to babysit Todd, Edgar headed to work, and Monique drove to Fairview Day Camp to watch the divers attempt to destroy the jumping fish.

Since the divers were scheduled to begin their assignment at nine-thirty, Monique arrived at the closed camp at nine o'clock. She wasn't alone. An attractive redhead stood on the edge of the shore talking to a cameraman and making broad gestures toward the water while a round-faced brunette in her late forties, dressed in cut-off jeans and holding a notepad, sat on the sand nearby watching them.

Monique approached the seated woman and held out her hand. "Morning. I'm Monique Atchison from *Weird World Weekly*."

"Hi," the woman said, smiling and shaking Monique's hand. "Felice Bellway. I'm a stringer for the *County Courier*. They told me to cover the divers this morning."

"Who's the redhead?" Monique asked, nodding towards the young woman, who was still talking animatedly to the man with the camera.

"Oh, that's Rachel Castell, ambitious Peachwood area reporter for WBTR-TV. Everyone knows that she's trying to get a network job in New York." Felice pointed to the lake. "And she thinks this is the story that's gonna do it for her."

"She may be right," Monique said. "My paper thinks it's hot shit." She turned to the parking lot. "Any sign of the divers?"

"Not yet. Things tend to move slowly around here."

"Yeah, seems that way," Monique said as she sat next to the woman and sifted grains of glittering sand through her fingers. "Heard any new information on the fish?"

"My editor at the *Courier* just said they'd be sending people into the lake this morning," Felice said with a shrug. "Sorry. That's really all I know. As a freelancer, I'm not in the loop."

"Then we'll just have to see what happens." Monique wiped some sand off her jeans and smiled.

—⚡—

"Todd, why'd you stop the game?" Kady asked, holding the soccer ball they had been kicking back and forth. Her young neighbor had walked to the edge of the backyard and was staring intently at the lake.

"Look at all the people over at Fairview." The boy pointed to a crowd of about twenty who had gathered on the opposite shore. "I heard my dad say divers were going into the lake this morning to kill the fish dead." He turned to Kady. "I wanna watch. Okay?"

The girl groaned. "Todd, we've been through this before. Remember, we tried to watch the boats on Thursday and we couldn't see anything that happened because we were too far away. And this is much further. It's all the way across the lake and the divers will be under the water so we won't see *anything*."

"Yeah, but if something bad happens, we'll know just like before," he said, smiling at Kady. "We can hear the screams."

"I don't want to hear people screaming! C'mon, Todd." She pulled his arm gently. "Let's finish the game before it gets too hot to play."

When the boy didn't move, Kady tried another tactic. "You know, these guys going into the lake today are professional divers. They're used to swimming in water and bringing back stuff." She remembered the two men finding Mr. Urloch's body last Monday, but didn't mention that gruesome fact to Todd. "I'm sure they'll have strong guns and everything so there'll be nothing to see 'cause they'll kill the fish."

The boy turned around and looked at her. "But I want to see them kill it dead. And if they don't, then there'll be lots of bad stuff happening and we'll get to hear it. Owww!" Grasping his chest, he staggered and moaned, pretending to be in great pain.

"Todd!" Still holding the soccer ball, Kady lowered herself onto the grass next to him.

—m—

By the time the divers arrived at the day camp, Monique and her fellow reporters had been joined on the shore by two police officers—Pete Malone and Diana Wilson—and a crowd of about fifteen Peachwood Lake residents. At nearly ten o'clock, the same two men who had retrieved Marty Urloch's body from Peachwood Lake the previous week, stepped out of their "Water Rescue Unit" white van. This time, however, they wore much heavier wetsuits. In fact, their suits, made of watertight neoprene rubber, were the thickest available—nearly one half-inch deep. They had been FedExed overnight by the manufacturer especially for the day's dive. Usually these wetsuits were worn to keep divers' bodies warm in especially frigid waters. Here the thickness was for added protection against the bites of the killer fish.

The two men waddled towards the water in their fins, air tanks on their backs, looking a bit uncomfortable in the thick new gear, which also included waterproof waist pouches. In their hands, the divers each carried a titanium spear gun. Just yesterday they had taken a condensed course on how to use the weapons since, until this morning, spear fishing had not been part of their job description.

The divers walked past one of the camp's rowboats, which had been moved from Fairview's dock several hundred yards away to the edge of the sandy beach. The police had again added a trolling motor and two muscular young officers sat in the boat, ready to aid the divers in case of an emergency. Then, as the crowd watched, the two men waded into the water to find and destroy the malevolent fish.

—m—

After ten minutes of waiting, Todd grew bored. "This stinks!" he said, turning to Kady. "Nothing's happening. Why aren't they doing anything?"

"I don't know. But like I said, even though we saw the divers go into the lake, we can't see anything else. They're underwater and far away so there's nothing at all for us to watch this morning." She picked up the ball and stood up. "C'mon. Let's go back to the game."

"All right," the boy said, making a face and kicking the grass. "But I really wanted to see them kill the fish dead. If they can't kill it, I will. Like this." Pretending he was holding a knife, Todd made a series of slashing motions with his arms.

—m—

The divers, Greg Eccheviera and Justin Marshall, swam side by side underwater towards the middle of the lake. Since they had been partners for more than a year, the two men were familiar and comfortable with each other's swim patterns. They had also developed a large number of hand signals—nearly thirty—which they had reviewed several times that morning. In addition, the divers had devised two simple signals for their police support crew. The men were to signal the shore approximately every fifteen minutes with one of them making a brief wave, which meant, "We're okay." If they had any problem, one diver would signal with a raised hand held straight up and the policemen in the boat would immediately motor to the spot of the signal and retrieve them.

Now, however, the two men had no problem. Although they swam rapidly, they were vigilant, carefully observing the underwater scenery for signs of their adversary. As always, Peachwood Lake was translucent and lovely. Many schools of small fish drifted by, often nibbling on the aquatic plants that covered parts of the sandy bottom and occasionally a small crustacean scurried along the lake's floor. *Like an ad for a peaceful scuba vacation,* Justin thought.

Then, slowly, the seascape began to change. First the divers noticed fewer and fewer fish. Although the greenery was still plentiful, the absence of fish made the water seem somewhat eerie. The crustaceans had disappeared too. And finally, there were no fish at all.

Greg pointed to his watch, telling Justin it was time to signal the shore that all was well. The two swam towards the surface together and Greg gave a brief wave. Then they headed back down to the bottom of the lake.

—m—

"So far, so good," Felice Bellway said to Monique when the diver gave his "okay" signal.

"Yeah, but they've only been in the water for a few minutes and we can't see what the hell's going on down there."

The two reporters sat at the edge of the shore with most of the crowd, staring at the lake, while Rachel Castell and her cameraman still stood nearby. Monique noticed Rachel was getting antsy. First the TV reporter took out a mirror and examined her hair and makeup. Then she checked her watch and grimaced. *Must have more important things to do,* Monique thought, chuckling to herself.

"Look, there's the jumping fish!" a woman shouted.

Glancing at the crowd, Monique saw a chubby woman in a loose tee shirt and baggy brown shorts pointing to a spot in the right side of the lake. Monique didn't see the fish, but she did notice a small eddy far out in the water. "How do we tell the divers where it is?" she asked Felice.

Felice shook her head. "I don't think we can. If they're attacked, let's hope they'll be able to kill it."

As the group on the day camp shore continued to watch—now

more alertly—the fish jumped again, this time a little further to the right. Several people pointed to it and whispered amongst themselves. Then, when nothing else happened, they resumed staring at the lake and waiting.

—⟋⟍⟍—

Unaware of the sighting on the shore, Greg and Justin swam near the center of the lake still not seeing any fish until—suddenly this time—the seascape changed once more. There were fish again—all of them dead. Scores of bodies of mutilated fish now covered the bottom of the lake. Some looked partially eaten, but most had been slashed, bitten, or hacked and then abandoned. "Not good," Greg signaled. Justin shook his head in agreement and indicated that he wanted to put a few of the dead fish into his pouch to take back to shore. Greg kept watch while his partner gathered the bodies.

The divers continued to swim through the dead-fish zone, now even more vigilant than they had been. *Like a giant lair of a sea monster*, Greg thought.

As both men noticed a sudden movement on their left, they turned and confronted their prey. What the divers first noticed were its teeth—the creature had so many, all of them big and sharp with serrated edges, almost like steak knives. *Fish looks like a gigantic mouth*, Justin thought as he quickly aimed his spear gun.

The spear struck the fish's body, but didn't penetrate at all, just bouncing off. The creature's skin was segmented and looked hard, not slimy. Justin wondered if it had some kind of armor plating instead of scales and skin. Quickly, he gave Greg their "Let's get the hell out of here!" emergency signal. But his partner wasn't paying attention to him; Greg was just treading water and staring dumbfounded at the fish so Justin grabbed the stunned man and began swimming rapidly towards the surface.

As the fish darted towards the two divers, Justin, still holding Greg, reached for his partner's spear gun and tried to aim it at the creature. But the fish lunged at the weapon, and, with one ferocious bite, cut it into two pieces. Then the creature swam upward and, in a single motion, chopped off Greg's air hose.

Before Justin could undo his air valve to share it with his partner, the fish attacked again, this time leaping at Greg's legs. Still in a daze, the man offered little resistance as the fish bit through the nearly half-inch thick neoprene rubber wetsuit and tore off a chunk of his thigh.

Oh God! Justin thought as he kept swimming upward. He could feel the fish continuing to bite his partner and knew there was nothing he could do except get to the surface as quickly as possible.

Finally, Justin reached the top of the water and raised his hand straight up—the prearranged signal for help. Then he turned Greg's face out of the water and stared at his partner. From the blank look in the man's eyes, he knew it was already too late.

—ɱ—

At the day camp, the people watching the water saw the diver's signal and the immediate action by the policemen in the rowboat, who motored as rapidly as they could toward the middle of the lake. The crowd, which now numbered more than thirty, attempted to move closer to the water's edge, but Officers Pete Malone and Diana Wilson pushed them back. Monique and Felice flashed their news media IDs and were allowed to remain nearer to the lake.

"One of them's hurt," Monique said to Felice, taking a pad and pen from her bag. "See how he's holding the other guy up."

Just then Rachel Castell sprung into action, moving so she stood with her back towards the water and holding her mike as the cameraman began filming. "This is Rachel Castell reporting live at Fairview Day Camp in Peachwood Lake, where during the last week, three people have died tragically, victims of a savage fish.

"I am standing here, waiting for police in a rowboat to pick up the two brave divers who went into the lake this morning to destroy the fish." She turned and, with her microphone, indicated the boat, which had reached the men in the water. "The divers just signaled that they had a problem. We don't yet know if the men were successful in killing the fish and we certainly hope and pray that they are both all right. The divers' names are..." Rachel glanced at a small sheet of paper she was holding. "...Justin Marshall and Greg Eccheviera." She paused for a moment. "This has been a devastating and tragic time for the small town of Peachwood. It all started last Monday when a man named Martin Urloch went fishing..."

"She's really milking this," Felice whispered to Monique.

"Yeah, I see."

As the two women watched, the officers in the rowboat helped one diver lift the other one out of the water. "Not good," Monique said, pointing to the limp body. "That diver's hurt real bad. He's either unconscious or worse." She and Felice stood quietly, listening to Rachel's commentary on the week's deaths and injuries in Peachwood Lake as they waited for the rowboat to return to the shore.

"Look! Something happened in the water." Todd threw the soccer ball on the ground and dashed to the edge of the lake. "There's a rowboat in the middle of the lake and..." He squinted to get a clearer picture. "I can see three people in the boat."

"Yeah, I kind of see them too," Kady said as she reached the boy. "But we can't see anything else. Then, when the boat gets back to the camp, they'll be even further away and we won't see anything at all." She put her arm around Todd's shoulder. "My friend Monique's there at the camp right now, watching everything. She's a great reporter and she's staying with me and my dad. When she comes back, she'll tell me everything that happened and I'll tell you too. I promise."

"Even if it's real bloody and gory like with Mr. Feinman?"

Kady sighed. "Yeah, okay. But only if you stop standing here and staring at the lake."

The boy smiled. "It's a deal. But I wanna talk to Monique too."

The rowboat motored into the camp's dock and Justin got out, holding Greg's broken spear gun and air hose. The two policemen carried his partner's body as carefully as they could, but blood dripped from many gaping wounds as the three of them walked through the sand to the parking lot. Officer Malone had called for an ambulance and the vehicle, with flashing lights on, had just pulled in, its engine still running.

It was a gruesome picture: Greg's left leg had been bitten to the bone and it dangled loosely from his torso. Several pieces of his wet suit had been gouged and the unprotected parts of his body had been savagely chewed, revealing jagged pieces of torn flesh, especially around the chest.

"Don't film the body!" Rachel shouted to her cameraman as the foursome approached. "We can't put that on TV! It's too disgusting for our viewers. Just show the cops carrying it and show the other diver." She picked up the mike and began talking rapidly. "The rowboat has landed, and, sadly, there has been another tragedy here in Peachwood Lake..."

Not too gross for my readers, Monique thought as she followed the sad procession. *They love this sick shit*. Using her digital camera, Monique snapped several photos of the mutilated diver, nearly gagging at the brutality of the attack.

"Ohhh...," Felice mumbled, putting her hand over her mouth and turning away from the body. Then, still holding her notepad, she ran to the edge of the water, retched, and vomited into the lake.

Rachel, having finished her summary, rushed over to Justin Marshall and shoved a microphone in the distraught diver's face. "I'm so sorry," she said. "Can you please tell me what happened to you and your partner just now in the lake?"

The diver glared at the reporter through tear-filled eyes. Angrily, he pushed the microphone aside, nearly knocking Rachel to the ground, and continued walking to the ambulance.

"The jumping fish!" a man shouted. "I see it! It's still there!" People turned away from the scene on the shore to look again at the water. Monique stared too. But all she saw was a small eddy near the middle of the lake.

CHAPTER 12

KILLER MONSTER LOOSE IN CONNECTICUT LAKE!

by Monique Atchison

PEACHWOOD, CONNECTICUT — Peachwood Lake, normally a beautiful crystal-clear oasis in this sleepy Connecticut town, has morphed into a deadly battleground. A modern sea monster now controls its suddenly treacherous waters. The murderous jumping fish—species unknown—has already killed four people in alarmingly brutal fashion, the latest victim just this Monday morning.

Diver Gregory Eccheviera, 29, was hacked to death by the evil creature. As the photos show, his left leg was nearly completely bitten off and his "protective" diving suit offered no protection. The monster was still able to chew through the material and tear out chunks of the victim's flesh.

Eccheviera and his diving partner, Justin Marshall, 31, had gone into Peachwood Lake armed with spear guns to destroy this murderous sea creature. Sadly, the two men did not succeed. Immediately after the incident, the fish—which has the ability to jump high into the air—was again seen leaping above the water. It is still in total charge of Peachwood Lake.

The monster has been described by witnesses as a four foot elongated-shaped fish with an armor-like body and many huge, razor-sharp teeth. So far, even after autopsies of the victims and examination of the bite marks, scientists have not been able to figure out the creature's identity.

Early Sunday morning, the fish mutilated Tiffany Terrizini—a strikingly beautiful 16-year-old—ripping apart the high-school student's heart...

Working on her laptop in the Peachwood library, Monique finished writing her article with a recap of last week's deaths, including as many of the gory details as possible. When she was done, she emailed the story, with the gruesome photos, to her editor. It would be posted on the *Weird World Weekly* website within the hour.

Then Monique returned to the Internet. She had some important research to do.

—⟋⟋⟍—

Todd saw a young African-American woman walking gracefully across Kady's backyard. "Is that your friend?" he asked, knocking over their Chutes and Ladders game as he rushed towards her.

"Yes," Kady said, picking up the board and fallen pieces from the grass. "But you don't have to run. Monique sees us and she's coming right over here."

Nevertheless, Todd kept racing until he reached the reporter. "What happened?" he asked. "Did the fish kill someone dead again? Who was in the boat?"

"Whoa." Monique held out her hand like a stop sign. "Slow down. First of all, Mr. Question Man, we haven't even met. It's polite to introduce each other before asking all those questions." She extended her hand to the boy. "Hi. I'm Monique. It's nice to meet you."

He quickly shook her hand. "I'm Todd. Now tell me what happened."

Monique smiled at Kady. "Looks like we've got a junior detective here," she said. "Kid keeps asking for information." She lowered herself onto the grass and Todd and Kady sat next to her. "All right. The people you saw in the boat were policemen bringing the divers back to shore." She patted the boy's head and spoke softly. "Yes, the fish did kill someone this morning—one of the divers."

"Not again!" Kady said, shaking her head and sighing.

"I knew it!" Todd shouted, jumping up. "Was there lots of blood? Did the fish bite him hard and..."

"Todd!" Kady yelled.

"What did I do?" the boy muttered. "I just wanna know what happened." He stared at the ground, pursing his lips and pouting.

"I'll just say that it wasn't pretty," Monique said. "No gory details for either of you. And I'll tell you that the fish is still alive because people saw it jumping after the rowboat landed. But if you want more info, you'll have to ask your folks."

"Okay," Kady murmured, figuring her father would let her watch the evening news. Todd, however, continued to pout.

Monique turned towards the girl. "I already wrote my first fish story at the library and emailed it to *Weird World*."

"Can I read it?" Kady asked.

"Later," the reporter said, hesitating briefly. "Remember that marine biologist you said came to see you last week?"

"Frank?"

"Yeah. You have his number, right?"

"He gave me his card. Why?"

"I'd like to talk to him. I've got some questions about this fish and I'm hoping he's got the answers."

Kady walked to her house, got the marine biologist's card, returned, and gave it to Monique.

"Wish me luck," Monique said, crossing the second and third fingers of her left hand. After moving several feet from Kady and Todd, she opened her cell phone and made the call.

"Hello," said a male voice.

"Dr. Margolies?"

"Speaking."

"Hi. My name is Monique Atchison and I'm a friend of Kady Gonzalez, the girl you questioned last week about the killer fish she saw in Peachwood Lake...Remember her?"

"Of course. Lovely young girl, and smart too."

"That's her," Monique said, smiling. "She gave me your number because I'm a reporter for a weekly newspaper and I'd like to come and talk to you about some ideas I have about that fish...Have you guys figured out what it is?"

"No. We're still stumped." Frank paused. "So if you've got a theory about the fish, I'd love to hear it."

"Is sometime this afternoon possible?"

"When would you be here?"

Monique checked her watch. "Is three o'clock okay?" she asked. That would give her an hour to review the material and jot down questions.

"Three o'clock's fine."

After getting directions, she said goodbye, and closed the phone.

Dr. Frank Margolies shook Monique's hand and ushered her

into his small messy office in the Connecticut State Labs' complex. "Sorry about all this," he said, removing a pile of papers from a side chair to make room for her to sit. "I just never seem to find the time to clean up."

"I know that problem," Monique said, laughing as she sat.

Frank lowered himself into the swivel chair behind his cramped desk and smiled at his guest. "So you mentioned that you work for a weekly paper. Which one?"

She grimaced. "It's not *Time* or *Newsweek*. I work for a shitty rag...*Weird World Weekly*."

"Oh."

The reporter spoke quickly. "Listen Dr. Margolies, everything you tell me will be strictly confidential. In my story, I'll just call you a 'scientific expert involved with the case.'" She smiled. "Is that okay?"

"No mention of my name or Connecticut State Labs?"

"Promise."

"All right," he agreed. "Now tell me, what have you found out about our fish?"

Monique opened her notebook and began talking. "I may work for a weird newspaper, but this fish is weird too and you guys can't seem to figure out what it is. Since witnesses have said the fish looks like it's made of armor, I tried googling 'armored fish' and then 'prehistoric armored fish.'" She looked up at Frank. "That's when I got the word 'placoderms.' Mean anything to you?"

"Placoderms were fish with armor on the front of their bodies and no teeth, just bony plates, that lived during the Devonian Period," the scientist said, shaking his head. "They've been extinct for millions of years."

"True," Monique agreed as she checked her notes. "But they were fresh-water fish and one of them, the Dunkleosteus, was a real sea monster. It even killed its own kind." She looked up. "And it lived in the Appalachian Basin. That's right around here."

"The Dunkleosteus was huge, about twenty feet long," Frank

explained. "The fish we're talking about, witnesses agree, is maybe four feet long." He gasped and put his head in his hands. "What am I talking about? Placoderms are extinct. They died out suddenly, hundreds of millions of years ago."

Monique turned the page of her notebook. "Dr. Margolies..."

"Please call me Frank."

"Okay, Frank," she said, skimming through her notes. "Isn't it true that sometimes fish that scientists thought were extinct are discovered to still exist? The coelacanth, for example."

"Yes, that's true. But instances like that are very rare."

She raised her head. "But couldn't it happen here? Couldn't some kind of placoderm have shown up in Peachwood Lake somehow—and that's why you guys can't identify it, because you're not looking for an extinct fish?"

Frank leaned back in his chair, closed his eyes, and remained quiet for nearly a minute. "That's very interesting," he finally said. "It's definitely way out in left field, but still very interesting." The scientist moved forward and leaned his elbows on the cramped desk. "I'm not an expert on prehistoric fish, but I'd like to check your theory. Maybe I can find a placoderm that's a better fit with the Peachwood Lake fish, though I'm sure none of them were mentioned as jumpers."

"How would anyone know if any placoderms ever jumped?" Monique asked. "There were no eyewitnesses, except maybe a T-Rex." She grinned. "Anyway, if that fish has been alive since the dinosaurs, it's a survivor, and it's real smart. Maybe it's made changes..."

"A mutation?"

"Yeah, that's the word. Is it possible?"

Frank shrugged. "If a placoderm's alive today, then anything's possible...Monique, give me your number, please. Let me do some quick research and I'll call you if I find a description of a placoderm that looked anything like our Peachwood Lake killer."

She gave Frank her business card and asked him to call her on the cell phone. "Hope you find something."

"Me too," the scientist said, shaking her hand.

—⟋⟍—

"So where are we going for dinner tonight?" Monique asked when she walked into the Gonzalez's kitchen shortly after five o'clock.

Edgar, who had just gotten home and was sitting at the table with Kady, smiled at the reporter. "I can make dinner and we can eat here," he suggested.

Monique shook her head and waved her forefinger. "Remember our deal? *I* take care of dinner...So where're we going?"

"I was just telling Dad that I wanted to watch the news tonight so I can see more stuff on what happened at the lake today because you wouldn't show me the pictures you took," Kady said, frowning.

"That's right," Monique agreed as she sat and turned to Edgar. "They're too gory. Footage of the dead diver won't be on TV either since the reporter who was there wouldn't even let her camera guy take them. But I want to see the news too, so how about let's go someplace for a quick meal. You guys choose the place."

"What about the pizza shop in the mall?" Kady asked.

"Fine with me," her father said.

"Give me a minute to wash up and then let's go," Monique said as she headed to the bathroom.

—⟋⟍—

The mall's lot was just half full when Edgar parked the Civic. However, when he, Kady, and Monique entered Tony's Pizzeria Plus, they found that the popular small restaurant in the middle of the shopping center was packed.

"Here's a table," Kady said, running to the only available seats and quickly claiming them. Monique and Edgar followed at a slower pace.

"Seems to be a good choice," the reporter said, scanning the room as she picked up the menu. "Lots of people usually means good food. What do you guys usually have?"

"Just pizza," Kady said. "But we haven't been here in a long time. We don't eat out much."

"Well, as long as I'm staying with you, you'll be eating out plenty."

Kady smiled and opened her menu.

"Maybe I'll try the veal marsala," Edgar said quickly. "I haven't eaten veal in years."

"Fine." Monique closed her menu. "And I'm gonna order the chicken parm. How about you, Kady?" She looked at her young friend.

"I still want pizza. They make it real good."

A gum-chewing teenage waitress wrote down their orders and left.

—m—

"Fraidy Kady."

The words weren't spoken loudly, but to the girl, the taunt sounded like a shout. Monique and her father were talking about their cars and gas prices—boring stuff—and Kady had tuned out. *They didn't hear it*, she realized, glancing at her dinner companions as they continued their two-way conversation.

The teasing words had come from somewhere behind her so, very slowly, Kady turned around. Two tables back, she saw Hannah and two of her friends sitting with their mothers. One of the girls noticed her staring at them, said something to Hannah, and pointed. Hannah smiled and either whispered or mouthed "Fraidy Kady" again. It didn't matter. Even without hearing the words, she still knew exactly what Hannah was saying.

Kady had really been looking forward to having pizza. Now she studied the silverware and didn't say anything, determined not to cry.

Edgar noticed his daughter seriously examining the plain white tablecloth. "Is everything okay?" he asked.

"Fine," she said, trying to sound normal. She glanced up and smiled, hoping her expression didn't look fake. "I just wasn't interested in all that car stuff."

"Sorry," Monique said. "Let's change the subject. What do you want to talk about?"

Kady heard laughter from Hannah's table and scowled.

"Hey, hon, that wasn't a tough question," Monique said, patting the girl's shoulder.

"Sorry." She tried to stop thinking about Hannah and her friends. "How about you tell us more about what happened today at the lake?"

"No. That's not dinner conversation. Choose something else."

"What about your trip to see Frank?" she asked, giving the reporter a questioning look. "You haven't even mentioned anything about that."

Monique shook her head. "No. That's a secret for now. You'll have to wait to read my story."

Before Kady could think of another topic, the waitress arrived with their dinners.

"You were right about this place," the reporter said after taking several bites of her chicken parmesan. "It's real good."

"And I had forgotten how delicious veal is," Edgar added.

Kady tried to enjoy her pizza, but she kept hearing Hannah and her friends talking and laughing behind her. She tried to convince herself that their conversation didn't have to be about her. Maybe they were just talking about something funny. Then she heard Hannah say those terrible two words again and she put down her slice and bowed her head.

"What's the matter?" her father asked. "Isn't the pizza good?"

"It's great," Kady said, forcing herself to smile. "I'm just not very hungry, that's all."

"But I thought you were looking forward to this dinner." He pointed his fork at the girl. "You're the one who asked to eat here."

"Yeah, I know. But I kinda lost my appetite."

"Are you feeling okay?" Edgar leaned over to touch his daughter's forehead. "Do you think you might be getting sick?"

She moved away so her father couldn't reach her. "No, I'm all right, just not hungry...Can I take the pizza home and eat it later?"

"Sure," Edgar said, patting her hand. Monique gave her a quizzical look, but didn't say anything.

Edgar and Monique quickly finished eating their dinners. When she got the check, the reporter asked the waitress to put the girl's two slices of pizza in a doggy bag.

As they left the restaurant, Kady was careful not to look at Hannah or the people at her table. But she couldn't escape the sounds of their laughter.

Immediately after returning home, Kady regained her appetite. She stood next to the kitchen counter and wolfed down her pizza while her father turned on the TV so they could watch the local news. Monique and Edgar sat on the loveseat and the girl finished her meal and then lay on the living room carpet.

"Good evening," the blond anchorman began. "Sadly, there has been another death in Peachwood Lake. This morning, diver Gregory Eccheviera was killed by the fish that he and his fellow diver, Justin Marshall, were trying to destroy." The newscaster sighed deeply. "Now, let's go out to Rachel Castell, who's been covering this story and is reporting live from the lake."

The scene switched to the pretty redhead, standing on the sandy beach of a now-deserted Fairview Day Camp, her back to the water. "Thank you, Rob. This is where Gregory Eccheviera lost his life earlier this morning." She turned around and pointed to the lake. "He and his partner swam to the middle of the water to kill the fish that has, in a short time, taken over Peachwood Lake. Here is some footage that we shot earlier, just when the rescue boat pulled to shore." The TV screen showed the rowboat landing, with one diver slumped over. The next picture showed Rachel asking the teary-eyed surviving diver to comment on what happened, followed by him angrily shoving her microphone out of his face and walking away.

"As you can see, Mr. Marshall was too distraught to talk to me right after the fish brutally murdered his diving partner. However, later in the afternoon, he released this statement." She held up a piece of paper and read it aloud.

"I am deeply sorry that our failure to kill the fish today cost Greg his life. Everyone underestimated the strength and power of the creature. I shot it with the spear gun, but the spear didn't even penetrate the fish's skin, which looked like it was made of armor. The fish's teeth are so powerful that they bit the spear gun in half and bit through Greg's extra-thick wetsuit and his air hose.

"We discovered that the creature has been terrorizing and killing the other fish in the lake. Swimming towards the middle, we saw fewer and fewer fish, then no fish at all. At the center of the lake, we found hundreds of dead fish, which had all been horribly bitten or slashed. I picked up a few of the bodies, which scientists are now analyzing. I also gave the police a detailed description of the killer fish, so maybe they will be able to figure out its species. I know I've never seen anything like it before."

Rachel folded the paper and looked up at the camera. "In other Peachwood Lake-related news, Mayor Turnbull will hold a press conference tomorrow at noon at Town Hall to announce the town's next plan for destroying the fish." She paused and nodded seriously at the screen. "Of course, I'll be there."

"I'll be there too," Monique said, jotting the information in her notebook.

"They didn't show any pictures of the diver who got killed," Kady complained.

"I told you, it was too gross," the reporter said.

"I know, but I thought they'd at least show something."

"Not appropriate for TV audiences." Monique shook her head.

"I'm glad they didn't show those pictures," Edgar said, muting the sound. "Now what do you two ladies want to do this evening?"

"I have a story to write," Monique said, standing and waving her notebook.

"I guess I could work on my story too," Kady said. She turned to her friend. "And you said I could read the one you already wrote."

"Yes, but without the pictures."

"You creative people go right ahead," Edgar said. "I'm just going to chill out and watch TV." He leaned back in the loveseat and turned on the sound.

—⟋⟍—

In Kady's room, Monique first checked her cell phone for messages. "I've got two calls from my editor," she said as she typed in her password. When she played back the calls, she smiled.

The girl lay on her bed, elbows up. "What was so funny?" she asked.

"Not funny, just good. Debbie said she loved the story I wrote today. It's been getting lots of hits and she's sorry it just missed the Sunday night deadline for our paper." Monique glanced at Kady. "We're on the newsstands early Monday mornings. The second message was just telling me about the press conference tomorrow. But we already know that from the news."

"Did you bring a copy of *Weird World Weekly* with you?"

"Why?"

"I'd like to read it."

"Why'd you want to read that shit?"

"If the paper's so bad, then why do you write for it?"

Laughing loudly, Monique walked to Kady, gave her a hug, and sat on the edge of the teen's bed. "Girl, when I got out of college, I wanted to work full-time as a reporter. But I couldn't find a job—believe it or not, *The New York Times* wasn't calling, begging me to write for them—so I just freelanced for a while. I wasn't even making enough money to pay my rent and then I saw an ad for *Weird World*..."

"Do you hate your job?"

"Hey, I'd rather work for a *real* paper, but it's not so bad. Some of the stories are fun to cover...And I can be a lot more creative than most reporters. The pay is good and *Weird World* does give me the chance to write regularly, with my byline." She squeezed Kady's shoulder. "And this job led to my meeting you, another very good thing."

The girl frowned.

"What's the matter? Meeting you was a good thing for me."

"Why? I'm nobody special."

"There you go again, putting yourself down." This time she shook the teen's shoulders. "Girl, you got to stop doin' that!"

Kady was silent for a moment. "Don't you have to write an article?" she finally said.

"Yeah, I told Debbie I'd have it by early tomorrow morning. How about you? You said something about writing a story, not a poem...Something new?"

"Kind of."

"Oh? What's it called?"

"'Mean Girls.'"

"Interesting title," Monique said. "Does it have anything to do with those girls at the pizza place tonight?"

Kady stared at her friend in shock. "You saw them?"

"Of course I saw them. I'm a reporter so I always notice things. I knew those girls were bothering you, but I don't know what they did to make you so upset that you couldn't eat your pizza."

"You didn't hear them laughing and giggling?"

"Yeah, I sure did." Monique nodded. "But girls your age always laugh and giggle." She smiled at Kady. "You're *supposed* to do that. It's part of being thirteen."

The girl lowered her head. "They were laughing at me," she whispered.

"How the hell do you know that? Their table was too far away for you to hear what they said."

"I heard enough."

"You got super hearing?"

"No...But I heard two words."

"And what two words did you hear?"

Kady spoke very quietly. "Fraidy Kady."

Monique considered the phrase. "Okay, let me try to put this together. Those girls tease you by calling you 'Fraidy Kady' over something you once did. Right?"

Kady nodded, her head still lowered. "Hannah does."

"And what was the terrible thing you did?"

"I got real scared by a spider in the bathroom in fifth grade and I screamed and Hannah saw me."

Monique hugged Kady tightly. "Oh honey, that girl's been on your case all this time?" she asked, lifting the teen's chin. "You're just too damn sensitive. Gotta not let her get to you 'cause she'll only stop teasing you if you stop getting upset. Here's what you have to do. Next time Hannah calls you 'Fraidy Kady,' imagine that she's standing there after having gone to the bathroom and a big piece of toilet paper's hanging out of her butt and trailing on the floor."

Kady laughed loudly.

"Good," the reporter said. "I see you've got the picture. Now just remember that for when you see that mean girl and her friends again."

"I'll try," Kady said, still smiling.

"I'm going to write my article now." Monique walked to Kady's desk and opened her laptop.

"You said I could read the one you wrote today."

"Sure. You can do that first and tell me what you think of it." The reporter switched on the computer and opened her Word documents.

Kady read the article while Monique checked her notes. "It's real good and you make all the stuff that happened sound very gross," Kady said. "But it would have been lots better with the pictures."

Monique smirked and punched the girl softly in the arm.

They spent the rest of the evening composing their very different stories. While Monique wrote her monster-fish article, Kady took out her notebook and pencil and worked on "Mean Girls":

Kathy was in the supermarket. All of a sudden, while
her aunt shopped in another aisle, a cart hit Kathy in the foot.

"*Ex-cuuse me,*" *Anna laughed.* "*Did that hurt you?*"

"*Yes,*" *Kathy said, rubbing her foot.*

"*Good!*" *Anna said.* "*Now get out of here or I'll do it again!*"

CHAPTER 13

LAKE MONSTER: A PREHISTORIC KILLER?

by Monique Atchison

PEACHWOOD, CONNECTICUT — The jumping fish responsible for the deaths of four people in this once-peaceful lake could be a placoderm—a real sea monster that lived in this same region hundreds of millions of years ago. Placoderms were armored fresh-water fish that flourished in the Appalachian Basin during the age of dinosaurs. Of course, these creatures have been extinct for a very long time.

But are they really? One scientific expert involved with the Peachwood Lake investigation isn't so sure. He thinks it's possible that the mysterious fish terrorizing lake residents today is related to the ancient placoderms. The scientist suggests the killer fish could be a mutation, having made changes throughout the years in order to be able to survive these many millenniums.

It's happened before that a fish thought to be extinct was found to still exist. The coelacanth is even called the "dinosaur fish" or "fossil fish" because a living one was discovered in the waters near South Africa in 1938—and coelacanths continue to survive today.

If the creature terrorizing Peachwood Lake is a kind of placoderm, let's hope it's not a Dunkleosteus....

Sitting in the Peachwood library early Tuesday morning, Monique reread her story and smiled. "Finally got my dinosaur," she murmured. Then she emailed the article, plus a picture she had found of a terrifying-looking Dunkleosteus with open jaws revealing fang-like bony plates, asking her editor to include it. Next, she clicked onto the Internet to do some more research.

—⟋⟍—

Monique was still at the library, investigating reports of strange fish sightings, when her cell phone rang. Dashing into an alcove, she took the call.

"Good morning, Monique," said a friendly male voice. "This is Frank Margolies. I've found something that I want both you and Kady to see."

"Really?" Monique whispered. "About what we talked about yesterday?"

"Yes...Very interesting stuff."

"Sounds great. Listen, I'm finishing up in the library and I can be back at Kady's house in just a couple of minutes. I'm staying there while I'm covering the fish story and I'm free till eleven-thirty this morning and Kady's next door babysitting. Can you come over sometime soon?"

"I'm getting in the car right now so I'll be there within half an hour."

"Thanks, Frank. See you then."

—ɯ—

The marine biologist rang the Gonzalez's doorbell at ten-thirty. "Glad to see you again so soon," Monique said, shaking his hand.

"Same here. Let's go get Kady." Frank waved the pile of papers he held in his left hand. "I want her to see this too."

After grabbing her shoulder bag, Monique locked the Gonzalez's cottage with the spare key Edgar had given her and she and the scientist walked to the Cimino's house. When they knocked, Kady peered through the peephole and then opened the door with Todd standing next to her.

"Why're you both here?" she asked, giving the two of them a puzzled look.

"I found something that I wanted to show you and Monique," Frank said. "Can we come in?" Glancing down, he smiled at Todd. "Hi. I'm a friend of Kady's."

"What's your name?"

"Frank." The scientist offered the boy his right hand. "And what's your name?"

"Todd," he replied, shaking the man's hand.

"Well, Todd, I've got some fish pictures here for Kady look at." Frank pointed to the papers in his left hand.

"Can I see 'em too?"

"Sure."

"This way." Todd smiled as he darted into the kitchen. After Kady moved the game of checkers she and Todd had been playing to the counter, the four of them took seats around the kitchen table.

"Okay, here's what I found," Frank said, pulling out one of the papers. "Kady, does this look more like the fish you saw?" The girl and the others stared at a picture of an elongated silver fish with armor plates covering the front half of its body.

Kady picked up the paper and examined it more closely. "Yes, it does," she said, nodding and pointing to the fish's mouth. "Especially those big sharp teeth."

"They're not really teeth," Frank explained. "They're bony plates. But this fish used them like teeth. Here, look at this." He placed another picture on the table, this one showing a close-up of a fish's jaw. "See how sharp these plates could be? This fish used its mouth like a pair of scissors, biting off pieces of its prey."

"Cool!" Todd said. He opened his mouth and snapped it shut noisily.

Monique tapped the jaw picture. "The fish's mouth looks like a set of steak knives...Look, it's even got serrated edges."

Frank nodded.

Kady put the first fish picture back on the table. "The only difference is the fish I saw in the lake had those patches of armor all over its body," she said. "Here too." She touched the lower end of the fish. "Otherwise, it's real close...What kind of fish is this?"

The scientist found another sheet of paper, this one covered with writing. "Here's where it gets interesting," he said.

"Is this going where I think it's going?" Monique asked, taking her notebook and pen from her bag.

"You bet." Frank smiled at her and then addressed Kady. "This fish is called a Coccosteus, a smaller relative of a monster Monique and I talked about yesterday called a Dunkleosteus. The Coccosteus was four- to five-feet long and it did live in lakes right around here." After staring at the paper again, he looked up. "But it lived here nearly four hundred million years ago." Then he paused dramatically before speaking again. "The Coccosteus has been extinct for millions of years."

Kady stared at him, a confused expression covering her face, while Monique scribbled quickly in her notebook.

"'Extinct' means this fish doesn't exist anymore," Frank explained to Todd. "It hasn't been alive since the time the dinosaurs roamed the Earth."

"Wow!" the boy shouted. "This fish's like a dinosaur—real old."

"But if it's extinct, then it can't be the fish that's in Peachwood Lake—right?" Kady asked Frank.

"That's what I told Monique when she suggested that our mystery fish could be a member of this extinct group." The scientist shook his head. "But now I'm not so sure."

Monique smiled as she continued to write.

"But if it is that Cocco-something fish and no one's seen it for millions of years, how did it get into Peachwood Lake?" Kady asked.

Frank shrugged his shoulders. "I have no idea."

"And how do we get rid of it?" Kady continued.

"I have no idea about that either," Frank said as Monique kept writing.

"Can't I just shoot it dead?" Todd asked, pretending his index finger was a gun. "Bam! Bam! Bam!"

Kady faced the boy and smiled at him. "It's got some kind of protection, like armor. Remember?"

"Oh yeah. I forgot." Todd dropped his finger-weapon.

Monique stopped writing, closed her notebook, and looked at all of them. "Well, we should get some idea of what the town plans to do about the fish in a few minutes," she said, glancing at her watch. "There's a press conference at noon and I'm going to be there." She dropped the notebook and pen into her oversized bag and stood up. "I'll let you know what they come up with...What're you going to do next about all this?" she asked Frank, indicating the pictures on the table.

The scientist picked up his papers and arranged them carefully. "I'm going to show these pictures to the diver and the police officers who were in Peachwood Lake," he said. "A couple of them had good close-up looks at the fish. Let's see what they say."

"And if they think it's the same fish..." Kady began.

"I'm not sure what'll happen." Frank shrugged. "We still need to capture the fish to see what it really is."

A dozen media people were already inside the brick Town Hall building when Monique arrived a few minutes before noon. She looked for Felice, the newspaper stringer she had met on Monday, but didn't see her. *Becoming too big a story*, Monique thought. *Paper probably sent a staff reporter.* Scanning the room, she spotted Rachel Castell in the front accompanied by the same cameraman who had been with her at the lake. Once again, the red-haired TV newswoman was busily gesturing orders to the photographer, who nodded continuously. "Man looks like a goddamn bobblehead doll," Monique muttered as she took a seat in the middle of the second row.

At noon, Mayor Turnbull, wearing a black pantsuit that was a size too small, walked to the podium, followed by Peachwood's four Town Board members, who took seats facing the audience.

"Good afternoon, ladies and gentlemen," the mayor began. "Unfortunately, I've had to call this meeting today because, as you all know, we have been unable to destroy the murderous fish that has been attacking people in Peachwood Lake. The Board and I met again yesterday afternoon, then in the evening, and yet again early this morning to work out a new plan of attack." She sighed. "It took a long time, but I think we've finally come up with a good solution. It may sound violent, but it's really not—and it's certainly better than the other, much more drastic measures that we've been considering." Removing her glasses, she wiped her forehead with her right hand. "We've decided to bomb the lake."

Most of the audience gasped and stared at the mayor in shock. "What the hell are you talking about?" a man yelled from the back of the room. "Are you freakin' nuts?"

"Hold on." Mayor Turnbull raised her left hand to stop the media's rumblings. "Let me explain. It's not at all what you think." She took a deep breath and tugged nervously at her suit jacket. "From what Mr. Marshall—the surviving diver—has told us, there are no live fish or marine creatures anywhere near the middle of the lake, just dead fish, so if we blast the center of Peachwood Lake, the only fish we're going to kill will be the murderous creature we are trying to destroy."

The mayor took another deep breath. "Obviously, we are going to be very careful here," she continued. "We've been working closely with the Air Force. They've already calibrated the right-size bomb and they're going to send a team to drop it. They have assured us that they will be able to position the bomb precisely in the middle of the lake. But, just to be on the safe side, we are still going to evacuate all residents whose homes border the lake in the event that the blast kicks up rocks or other debris that could shatter windows or do any minor damage to houses." She stared at the stunned audience. "We don't expect any problems, but we don't want anyone near the lake, just in case."

She unfolded a sheet of paper and glanced at it. "The bombing of the lake will take place tomorrow morning at precisely ten a.m. This afternoon, we will send police officers with notices to inform all affected residents, and if residents are not home, we will leave these notices attached to their front doors. Tomorrow morning at nine o'clock, members of the National Guard will escort Peachwood Lake residents to safety before this bombing plan is carried out. The Air Force has told us that this whole operation should be very quick, lasting only five or ten minutes."

She smiled weakly at the members of the media. "Now I'm sure you have some questions."

Rachel Castell immediately raised her hand and the mayor nodded to her. "Yes, Rachel," she said, still smiling.

"Mayor Turnbull, we all realize what a difficult situation this is," Rachel began. "But don't you think bombing the lake is rather extreme?"

"No." The mayor shook her head. "Actually, it's not. The other solutions we've been considering are much more extreme."

After looking at the other raised hands, the mayor pointed to a thin young man with a goatee. "Go ahead, Jake."

"What about sending professional fishermen into the lake?" the *County Courier* reporter asked. "I mean, it is still just a fish. Can't we just try to catch it?"

"No, we can't," Mayor Turnbull said. "We're not risking any more lives so we're not sending more people in boats into the lake. We've already gone that route and it hasn't worked."

The mayor gazed at the audience and selected a middle-aged woman, wearing a bright pink blouse.

"I know you said you don't expect to harm any other fish," the woman began. "But you can't be sure of that. What if the bomb is more powerful than you expect and does kill some of the fish that are still alive in the..."

"Please," Mayor Turnbull interrupted. "I'm as much of an animal lover as anyone in this room." She held up both hands and used her fingers to count. "I've got two dogs, one cat, three hamsters, and a cockatoo, so I really do understand your point of view...However, we're talking about fish versus people here and people are more important. If we have to sacrifice some fish in order to save the lives of innocent people, so be it."

The mayor looked at the raised hands again and indicated a dark-skinned man with glasses.

"What about the jumping fish?" he asked. "Didn't you want to catch it in one piece so that scientists could examine it to figure out exactly what it is? From what I understand, they still don't even know its species. So now you're going to blow it up and it'll be totally mutilated, making it impossible to find out what kind of fish it was."

The mayor nodded her head in agreement. "You're absolutely right. If this bomb works, we won't be able to determine the fish's species and, in terms of scientific knowledge, I am truly sorry about that. But I repeat, our main priority is to protect our citizens, and, to do that, we have to destroy the murderous fish. It's too bad we can't kill it in one piece, but..."

She shrugged, stared at the audience, and pointed to a disheveled-looking man in his early thirties wearing a New York Giants tee shirt. "Yes?"

"Where do we go tomorrow to watch the lake bombing?"

he asked.

"Good question," Mayor Turnbull said. "The press will be able to witness the bombing of the lake at the grounds of Fairview Day Camp. Since, as you all know, the town's lakefront area is very small, Stan Feinman's widow, Gloria, has graciously given us permission to use the camp as our headquarters, so you will all be able to view the explosion from there."

She glanced at her paper. "The Air Force said that you'll have to stand twenty feet back from the shore. The National Guard will be there to determine the exact distance."

The mayor scanned the room again. "Next." She pointed to a heavy blonde woman in the back row.

"I'm Charlene Frommage with the Ecological Protection Patrol," the woman said, standing and folding her arms over her massive chest. "I must protest your decision. You've made an absolutely horrible choice. Setting off any kind of bomb will be devastating to the vegetation in the water, even if you say the sea creatures won't be harmed. Have you even considered what will happen to the plant life in the lake when a bomb is exploded?"

"No, frankly we have not," the mayor replied. "While I'm all for protecting the environment, right now, as I've been saying, our primary goal is to protect our citizens and to do that we have to get rid of the fish that's been killing them." She pushed her glasses against the bridge of her nose. "Unfortunately, we may have to damage some plant life along the way. I apologize in advance for that, but we're still going to bomb the lake."

Mayor Turnbull stared at the audience. "Any other questions?"

Monique raised her hand.

"Go ahead, please," the mayor said.

"What if the bomb doesn't kill the fish?" Monique asked. "Then what'll you do next?"

Mayor Turnbull frowned. "This plan should work," she said. "The Air Force has assured us that it will...We don't want to have to consider the other drastic alternatives." She shook her head. "Anything else we do will totally destroy the lake."

She glanced around the room; no other hands were raised. "This meeting is over," the mayor said, gathering her notes. "Wish us luck tomorrow." Then, quickly, she turned and walked away from the podium.

CHAPTER 14

TOWN TO BOMB MONSTER FISH!
by Monique Atchison

PEACHWOOD, CONNECTICUT — Question: How do you destroy a killer fish that has been terrorizing your beautiful lake? Answer: Bomb the lake.

That's the solution chosen by officials in this normally peaceful little town. In a noon press conference Tuesday, Peachwood Mayor Margaret Turnbull announced that an Air Force team will drop a bomb in the center of Peachwood Lake Wednesday morning at 10 a.m. Town officials believe the blast will kill the monstrous jumping fish that has been responsible for the deaths of four people...

Working on her laptop in the Peachwood library, Monique continued her story by explaining the town's reasoning for deciding to bomb the lake, summarizing the information about placoderms she had discussed with Frank, and adding his new findings about the Coccosteus. Then she reviewed each of the gruesome Peachwood Lake deaths. "Can't have too many stories about dead people, especially folks who've been bitten to death," she muttered.

When Monique finished, she surfed the Internet for a good picture of a bomb blast over water, found one, and emailed it with her story to *Weird World*. "Debbie will love all this," she murmured.

—m—

After leaving the library, Monique sat in her car and called Frank. "How'd it go with your pictures?" she asked.

"Well, the police officers were being briefed on some upcoming assignment, so the only person I was able to talk to was the man who got hurt...Let me check his name." He didn't speak for a few moments and Monique heard the rustling sound of papers being shuffled. "Harry Conklin. He's on desk duty because of his injury."

"And...?" Monique was becoming impatient.

"And he basically confirmed what Kady told us. Officer Conklin said the picture of the Coccosteus looked very much like the fish that attacked him, except that the fish in Peachwood Lake had segmented armor-like pieces covering its whole body, not just its head area."

"What about the teeth?"

"He agreed that the Peachwood Lake fish had huge, pointed, and extremely sharp teeth. In fact, he opened his bandage and showed me the wounds—really deep cutting bites—and they did look very much like teeth marks. That confirms what we've seen on the dead bodies, and on the mutilated fish that the diver brought back. All the bites were made by extraordinarily sharp teeth."

"Speaking of the diver, have you talked to him yet?"

"No. I'm still trying to track the man down. No one's sure exactly where he is right now. Apparently, after what happened yesterday, he took the rest of the week off." Frank sighed. "I certainly don't blame him."

"Me neither. He really must've gone through hell." Monique

hesitated. "You mentioned the police had an upcoming assignment. I think I know what..."

"That's right," Frank said, interrupting the reporter. "You were at the town's press conference. What plan did they come up with?"

"They're going to bomb the lake."

"What?"

"You heard right. They're bombing the lake tomorrow. They think the explosion will kill the jumping fish."

"What about all the other fish?"

"They're dropping the bomb in the center of the lake where, from what the diver said, there are no other fish right now except dead ones. The Air Force is going to do the bombing, so the blast's supposed to just affect the middle area."

"Sounds pretty radical."

"I guess they know what they're doing," Monique continued. "Anyway, what I started to say is the town's going to evacuate all the people with homes right on the lake, just in case the explosion kicks up rocks or sticks that could break windows or do other damage and the police will be knocking on doors this afternoon to let people know. I bet that's what the briefing was about."

"Probably...They're really going to blast the lake?"

"Yeah, they are."

"You realize that if this bomb works, we'll never know the identity of the fish."

"No, we won't. But the town will have its lake back."

"True. But as a scientist, I'd really like to know what type of fish it is."

"As a reporter, I'm curious too, Frank. But I'd like to know what type of fish it *was*." After asking him to call her if he reached the diver or found out any new information about the fish, Monique ended the call.

"Hi, Kady."

Kady and Todd were kicking a soccer ball in the boy's backyard when she heard her name being called. Looking up, Kady saw a policeman walking towards them and recognized Officer Malone, whom she had spoken to last week when her neighbor, Martin Urloch, was killed. "What's wrong?" she asked.

"Nothing right now," Pete Malone said. "I'm walking around the lake this afternoon, making sure everyone gets this." He handed her one of the papers he was carrying.

"What's it say?" Todd asked, standing on his toes in an attempt to read the words of the flyer Kady now held.

"Hi," Pete said, ruffling the boy's hair. "What's your name?"

"Todd. This is my house." He pointed to his chest.

"I figured that, Todd, so here's one for you too," the officer said, handing him a paper.

The boy looked at the sheet. "Most of these words are too hard. I can't understand them." He turned to Kady. "All I can figure is they're gonna do to something to the lake. What?"

"They're going to bomb it," she whispered.

"Like in the movies?"

"Yeah, I guess." The girl shrugged.

"Not quite like that," Pete said. "Tomorrow morning, the Air Force is going to drop a small bomb in the middle of the lake to kill the jumping fish."

"A plane and a bomb! Neat!" Todd yelled. "Can I watch?"

"No," Kady said, shaking her head. "They're going to move us away from the lake so we don't get hurt."

"That's right." Pete nodded. "But you'll certainly be able to hear the blast."

"Boom!" Todd shouted, lifting his arms high above his head. "Awesome! I bet there'll be lots of waves and stuff..."

"What about the other fish in the lake?" Kady asked. "Won't they get killed?"

"They don't think there are any living things in the middle of the lake anymore except for the jumping fish," Pete explained. "They're trying to just aim for the center so the explosion doesn't damage too much else."

"Can they really do that?" she asked.

The policeman shrugged. "I don't know enough about bomb blast procedures. But the mayor says the Air Force can be very precise." He stared at Kady. "You never called me last week. Are you doing okay?"

"Yeah. I'm babysitting every day now since Todd's camp closed and I've got a friend, a reporter, who's staying with us."

"Covering the fish story?"

"Yes."

"Glad things are okay," Pete said, patting Kady's hand. "Remember, you can always call me if you need anything or just want to talk. Do you still have my number?"

"Thanks. I do."

After saying goodbye to Kady and Todd, the policeman walked to the next house on his route.

—◊◊◊—

Kady, Monique, and Edgar decided to eat dinner Tuesday at a local Chinese restaurant and Monique drove them to the small unpretentious eatery. Even though the meal consisted of several courses, they were finished in less than an hour. The reporter checked her watch. "It's still early and I don't have a story to write tonight. How about we go see a movie?"

"Shouldn't we go back to my house and watch the news?" Kady asked.

"Nah, we already know about the lake bombing," Monique said. "Nothing's gonna happen till tomorrow morning."

Edgar leaned back in his chair, hands on his stomach. "I haven't seen a movie in years," he said.

"There's a new Batman movie playing right here," Monique said. "I noticed it today while driving through town. We can get there just before it starts." She looked at her dinner companions. "So how about it, folks?"

Kady grasped her father's hand. "It might be fun, Dad," she said.

"If you two want to go, it's okay with me," Edgar said. "But drop me off at the house first. I'd rather just relax and watch TV."

Monique paid the check, they all got into her Elantra, and she drove Edgar home. Then she and Kady headed to the Peachwood Cinema.

—m—

Monique insisted on paying for Kady. "It was my idea and it's my treat. Remember, I'm the one with the expense account."

After the reporter bought a large tub of popcorn, the two of them entered the semi-dark movie theater while the previews were flashing on the screen and found seats on the far right side towards the front. Monique offered popcorn to Kady who took a handful.

As she munched her popcorn, Monique scanned the theater. "Crowded, huh? Movie got great reviews. Five stars." She grabbed a few more kernels and tossed them into her mouth.

Kady turned around and glanced at the people behind her. Immediately, she saw Jared, a boy she knew, and two of his friends, three rows back. Hoping the boys didn't see her, she tried to slink lower into her seat.

"What'cha doing way down there?" Monique asked.

"I just like to get real comfy when I go to the movies," the girl lied. "Sort of like I'm watching while I'm laying down in bed."

"Uh huh," the reporter said sarcastically. "Sure you do."

"Yeah, really. I'm just getting comfy."

"You don't look very comfy."

Kady folded her arms defiantly. "Well, I am."

Just then, the movie began, ending the conversation. Kady was relieved she didn't have to make up any more lies. The film was so entertaining that she soon forgot about the boys behind her and began inching up in her seat. By the time the movie ended—to enthusiastic applause and whistles of approval from the audience—she was fully upright.

"Wow!" Kady said, still clapping as she jumped up. "Great movie, Monique. Thanks so much for taking me."

"You're welcome," the reporter replied, stepping into the aisle. "Glad to do it."

As they neared the exit, Kady saw Jared and his friends just ahead of them. "Hold on a second," she said, abruptly standing still. "I think I got something in my sneaker."

Monique moved to the side of the aisle and stood next to the girl, letting the crowd pass while Kady slowly removed her shoe and shook it.

The three boys moved completely out of Kady's sight. "Okay, it's gone now," she said, relacing her sneaker. Without further conversation, they left the theater and got into Monique's red car.

—⚉—

"So what was that all about?" Monique asked as she drove to the Gonzalez's house.

For a moment, Kady didn't speak. "What do you mean?" she finally said.

"You know what I mean. All that shit at the movies—the crawling way down in the seat, the pebble in the shoe bit?"

Kady didn't reply.

"It was those boys behind us, right?" Monique continued.

"How'd you know?"

"I told you, girl. I'm a reporter. It's my job to notice everything. Now which boy were you trying to avoid?" Monique held the steering wheel with her left hand and used the fingers of her right hand to count. "The fat one, the tall one with glasses, or the long-haired one?"

"The tall one with glasses," Kady said, speaking softly.

"Why? Those boys didn't do anything mean to you. No whispers or giggles like those nasty girls."

"I'm afraid if Jared sees me, he'll make fun of me."

"But why?" Monique spread out her right hand. "There's nothing wrong with you. You're not dumb or ugly."

"I've known Jared since first grade and we used to be friends when we were kids. But when we got to middle school, he stopped talking to me."

"What about you? Didn't you stop talking to him too?"

"Yeah, I guess so...I guess maybe we both stopped talking."

The reporter nodded her head. "Yeah, that happens a lot. You get kinda shy around each other. You're scared of him and he's scared of you."

"Why would he be afraid of me?"

"You're a girl...And teen girls are scary to teen boys."

"I'm hardly a teen. And look at me." Kady pointed to her chest. "I'm so flat."

Monique laughed. "Oh, the boob issue. Yeah, I remember." She caressed the girl's shoulder. "Don't worry. You'll get them. I had a friend—her name was Gina—who was completely flat-chested until she turned fifteen. Then, suddenly, she became a D-cup. Real big ones." Monique indicated the size with her right hand. "Like melons." She chuckled. "But they were too big. Poor girl couldn't even stand up straight. Boobs kept pulling her down."

Kady smiled. "You're just making that up."

"Uh uh." Monique raised her hand in a swearing motion. "True story. But what I'm trying to tell you is to stop looking at yourself so negatively. You're cute, you're smart, and you're fun. If you give yourself a chance, and talk to other kids, you'll see that they'll like you—and you'll like them too. But you've got to get out there and try." She pulled in front of the Gonzalez's house and turned off the ignition.

Kady shook her head sadly. "It's too scary."

—m—

When Kady and Monique entered the cottage, they found Edgar comfortably nestled in the upholstered living room chair, watching a baseball game. "How was the movie?" he asked.

"Great!" Kady replied.

"Lots of superhero action stuff," Monique added, smiling.

"Do you two ladies have a show you want to see?" he asked, pointing to the television.

"That's okay, Dad. You're enjoying the game." Kady looked at Monique. "Unless you want to watch something on TV."

"No, thanks." The reporter smiled at Edgar. "Enjoy."

"I'll go to my room and write," Kady said. "Plus I want to read Monique's last article." She turned to her friend. "Can I?"

"Sure. Let's go."

They walked into Kady's room and the girl closed the door. Then she stood in front of the mirror over her desk, made a face, and sighed.

"What's wrong now?" Monique asked, sitting on her bed.

"I don't like my hair," Kady said, sticking out her tongue.

"Why not? Check out all those waves." Reaching over, she twisted a strand of the girl's dark brown hair around her finger.

"You've got all those great curls." Kady pointed to Monique's flowing black ringlets. "Your hair really stands out." The girl untied the rubber band that kept her shoulder-length tresses out of her face. "My hair's nothing special."

Monique put a hand on her chin and stared at Kady. "Let's see what we can do to make you like it better." She hesitated briefly. "How about bangs?"

Kady glanced at herself in the mirror. "That could work," she said, smiling.

"You got a good scissor I can use?"

Tilting her head, the girl looked at Monique. "When did you learn to cut hair?"

"In college. I cut my roommate's hair."

"Did you do a good job?"

Monique chuckled. "I must have. Vanessa asked me to cut it again."

Kady found a sharp pair of scissors in the kitchen and Monique spread a few newspaper pages on the bedroom floor. Then the girl sat in the desk chair while, slowly and carefully, her hairdresser created bangs.

"What do you think?" Monique asked when she had finished.

Kady studied her reflection in the mirror. "I like it." She shook her head back and forth and smiled. "It makes me look different, a little more grown up. I'm going to show my dad."

She returned a short time later.

"What did he say?" Monique asked.

"He said he liked the bangs." Kady smiled. "But he always says he likes everything about me." Gazing at the laptop, she turned to the reporter. "Can I read your story now?"

"Sure. And, this time, you can see the photo too."

After reading Monique's article, Kady took out her notebook and pencil and began writing a new "Mean Girls" scene:

> *It was Saturday afternoon. Kathy was at the movies with her aunt when she heard a girl laughing behind her. She turned around and saw Anna and two of Anna's friends. They were three rows back, sitting with three boys. One of them was Jason. Anna tapped Jason on the shoulder and pointed to Kathy.*
>
> *As Kathy slunk down into her seat, she heard the girls and boys behind her laughing even louder...*

CHAPTER 15

"Are you sure you're going to be okay this morning?" Edgar asked Kady early Wednesday. "I'm sorry, but I have to go to work." He shrugged and took a sip of coffee.

"I told you, Dad, I'll be just fine." Kady lowered her cereal spoon and leaned back in the chair. "People are gonna be here to move us away from the lake." She took a bite and then looked up. "I forget who they're sending."

"The National Guard," Monique said as she entered the kitchen. She poured a cup of coffee, sat at the kitchen table, and faced Edgar. "Kady's right, you know. Nothing will happen to her. She and Todd will be taken to another street, far away from the explosion."

"I worry about her though, here alone all the time," he said, sighing.

Kady threw down her spoon. "I am not alone!" she shouted. "I'll be with Todd and his parents are both okay with going to work today."

"All right," Edgar said. "But please be careful."

"Dad!"

—m—

Just before nine o'clock, two young men dressed in green and brown camouflage uniforms knocked on Todd's door. "National Guard!" the shorter man announced, flashing his ID as Kady peered through the peephole. "You know about the bomb this morning, right?" he said when she opened the door.

"Pow!" Todd made a booming sound and spread his hands out wide. Kady nodded.

"Anyone else here?" the tall, heavier man asked her.

"No."

"Okay then," he continued. "You kids gotta get outta here now. Follow us."

Kady took her pocketbook, grabbed two bottles of water from the refrigerator, and locked the front door. Then she and Todd followed the two men into the street.

"Hello, Kady and Todd," Mrs. O'Hara said as the children joined several of their neighbors.

Todd smiled at the petite widow who also lived next door to Kady.

"Hi, Mrs. O'Hara," the girl said.

"Some adventure, huh?"

Kady nodded.

As the small group continued along the street, the National Guardsmen pounded on two other doors. In the first house, they got no response. In the second home, a young blonde woman, wheeling a little girl in a stroller, joined the procession.

Heading away from the lake, the group climbed two uphill blocks until they reached Summit Street, where Kady, Todd, and their immediate neighbors joined a larger congregation of people, including several more National Guard members. Kady heard loud noises coming from her right. Turning, she saw about ten people, mostly women, carrying signs and walking in a circle, chanting the words, "No Bomb!" over and over. As the protesters walked, she was able to read the magic-marker wording on their handmade signs: "BOMBS KILL – FISH ARE

LIVING CREATURES!"; "DON'T DESTROY OUR LAKE!"; "BOMBING IS <u>NOT</u> A SOLUTION!"; "SAVE THE LAKE—DON'T BOMB IT!"

"This is cool!" Todd said. "Look!" He pointed to a red-haired woman, holding a microphone, who had positioned herself on the other side of the chanting group.

Following Todd's finger, Kady recognized the TV reporter, Rachel Castell.

"I am live this morning on Summit Street, a few blocks away from Peachwood Lake," Rachel began. "This is where the National Guard has assembled those residents whose homes are situated right on the lake and could be in danger of being hit by falling debris from this morning's bomb blast." She indicated the small circle of people holding signs. "As you can see, there's a group of protesters marching here. They've been chanting the words, 'No Bomb!' as they walk." She shoved the microphone into the face of the closest marcher, an overweight brunette with bright red lipstick. "Excuse me. Can you tell me why you are here today?"

"Bombing is never the answer," the woman said, lowering her sign. "All it does is destroy things."

"But don't you want to destroy the killer fish?" Rachel asked.

"Yes, but this is not the way."

"Do you have a better solution?"

"No." The woman shook her head sadly. "But I'm sure there is one."

"Thank you," Rachel said. The woman stepped back into the circle and continued to walk and chant.

—⟋⟍—

At the entrance to Fairview Day Camp, Monique showed her press pass to the pimply-faced young woman wearing National Guard camouflage and she was ushered into a small roped-off section right behind the beach.

"Hi there," Felice Bellway said, walking towards her and smiling. "Monique, right?"

"Yeah. Hi, Felice. You here reporting for the local paper again? I missed you at the press conference yesterday."

"Actually, I'm working my second job today. *Courier* has its staff guy, Jake Ellsbury, handling this." Felice pointed to the young man a few feet away from them who was talking on his cell phone. Then she shrugged. "Fish story's getting too big." She held up her camera. "I also do freelance photography for the local weekly so I hope I can get a good shot of the blast...How're you doing?"

"Been writing daily stories on all this shit for our website. So far, so good. My editor loves all the blood and guts." Monique scanned the media crowd. "Where's that hotshot TV reporter, Rachel...?"

"Rachel Castell? Oh, I'm sure she's around here somewhere because you know she would never miss this. They've moved all the people who live along the lake up to Summit Street." Felice nodded directly behind where she and Monique stood. "She's probably over there doing a human interest story. But you better believe she'll be back here in time for the bomb."

—*m*—

"Are you two kids here alone?"

Turning around, Kady faced another of her neighbors. "Hello, Mrs. Winzinski," she said, forcing a smile. "It's okay. We'll be fine."

"Are you sure?"

The girl nodded.

"Well, if you need me, I'll be right over here," Mrs. Winzinski said, indicating a group of four women in their fifties and sixties.

"Thank you." Kady smiled again.

"Bye," Todd said, waving as the woman returned to her friends.

Surrounded by the large crowd of evacuees, Kady and Todd stood on Summit Street and waited for the explosion. "I hear the plane!" the boy suddenly shouted.

Kady listened and, a few seconds later, she heard the sound too.

"There it is!" Todd yelled, pointing to a strange-looking plane heading in their direction. "What kind of plane is that? It looks more like a helicopter." He made a few whirring noises and spun himself around in a circle.

"I don't know," Kady said, gazing at the two rotary blades mounted on a rectangular shaft across the plane's body.

As she and Todd watched, the plane reached the lake and, like a helicopter, slowly began circling the water.

Kady took the boy's hand and attempted to hold it. "This could be real loud," she explained. "I don't want you to get scared."

Wrenching his hand free from Kady's grip, Todd gave the older girl a quizzical look. "Loud noises are cool. Boom!" He imitated the sound of an explosion, causing people to turn around and stare at him. "Why would I get scared? I never get scared."

Kady rolled her eyes. "Just watch the plane, Todd. Don't make any more bomb noises."

"Okay...Look the funny plane's coming closer." He pointed above the water. "I bet they're gonna drop the bomb now." He and Kady stared at the sky and waited.

—∿—

"Ever see a plane like that?" Monique asked Felice as the twin rotors hovered over the center of Peachwood Lake.

"Uh uh." Felice shook her head.

"I'm gonna check it out."

Then as she, Felice, and the rest of the media people watched, cameras in their hands, the Air Force plane released the bomb and, with jet-like speed, flew quickly away.

A thunderous noise reverberated through the air, causing both Monique and Felice to wince and instinctively hunch their shoulders to try to protect their ears as they hurriedly snapped photos of the blast. Waves splashed over Fairview's beach, kicking up a momentary dust storm of millions of granules of white sand. Most of the media crowd partially covered their eyes, squinting so they could still see and photograph what was happening. As they watched, the water reached the grassy area directly behind the camp building, spewing out mangled pieces of aquatic plants before the waves finally retreated.

"Look!" Felice shouted. She pointed to her left, by the lake's shallow end, where several fish seemed to have jumped out of the water. But, unlike the killer fish, these creatures didn't leap back in again. Instead, they lay unmoving, floating in the same spots where they had landed.

"Poor innocent fish," Monique muttered, shaking her head as she snapped a picture of the sad scene. "We know those little guys felt the blast. Let's hope the bomb got the damn killer fish too."

"Yeah," Felice agreed, lowering her camera. "You think it worked?"

Monique shrugged. "I don't know. It sure sounded powerful enough, but nothing's worked so far. I didn't see any big silver fish jumping in the middle of the lake so we'll just have to wait and see what happens." She lifted her hand and waved. "I gotta go. Got a story to write...See ya." As Felice nodded, Monique began walking towards the street.

"I'm standing here live at Fairview Day Camp where I have just witnessed the bombing of Peachwood Lake..."

Turning towards the loud female voice, Monique saw Rachel Castell facing the lake as she gave her TV report. "Guess she made it back here in time," Monique murmured as she slid into her car and drove to the library.

CHAPTER 16

PEACHWOOD LAKE BOMBED!
Is the Killer Fish Dead?
by Monique Atchison

PEACHWOOD, CONNECTICUT — On Wednesday morning, the V-22 Osprey—a helicopter-like Air Force plane—dropped a bomb into the middle of Peachwood Lake. The explosion created a powerful blast that rattled eardrums, produced ten-foot waves, damaged lake vegetation, and killed some innocent fish. But was it strong enough to destroy the mysterious jumping creature that has murdered four people and taken total control of this formerly peaceful lake?

Right now, officials can't be sure the bomb killed the one fish it hoped to destroy. They will just have to wait and see. If the fish is indeed dead, Peachwood residents will have their lake back. But if the ferocious lake monster begins jumping up and down in the water again, what will this small town do next?

Destroying the killer fish might be easier if the town knew exactly what type of creature it was fighting. But, so far, scientists have been unable to figure out its identity. One scientific expert involved in the investigation thinks the fish resembles a Coccosteus, a ferocious armored fish with razor-sharp plates instead of teeth. Only problem is the Coccosteus has been extinct for millions of years...

Monique finished the article by recounting her theory that the jumping fish might be related to the prehistoric placoderms. Then she again summed up the four gruesome murders, including all the gory details. After attaching a photo of the explosion and another showing the aftermath with the floating dead fish, she emailed her story to Debbie at *Weird World Weekly*.

—〰—

"What happened to the lake?" Todd asked Kady as they walked back to their house with a group of neighbors, again accompanied by the same two National Guardsmen. "I couldn't see anything."

"That was the idea," the girl explained. "That's why they moved us away. We weren't supposed to be right next to the lake in case some rocks or stuff came loose and hit us."

"At least I heard the bomb and it was real loud." Standing still, Todd spread his arms out wide and let out a deafening yell. "Boom!"

Several neighbors turned around and the group's taller escort smiled at the boy.

Kady, however, was not amused. "Todd, stop it!" she ordered. "That's enough screaming."

"We shoulda been able to see what happened," the boy grumbled, kicking some pebbles as he walked.

They reached the Cimino's house, waved goodbye to the National Guardsmen, and Kady unlocked the front door.

"I wanna go see what the bomb did," Todd said, immediately racing into the backyard.

"Just wait for me." Kady rushed after him.

The boy reached the edge of the water and stared at the lake. "It looks the same," he said, sounding disappointed.

"What did you expect?"

"I dunno...Maybe lots of dead fish on the grass and messed up rocks, sticks thrown all over the ground...Stuff like that."

Kady scanned the water. "I think there are some dead fish floating over there," she said, pointing to her left. "And the ground's real wet here." She lifted her sneakers and put them down gingerly. "See how squishy it is? So the water must have reached all the way out to here." She took a few soggy steps and picked up something green and slimy. "Look at this." She shoved the mushy green stalk near Todd's face. "I think this plant used to live in the water. See, it's all wet. The bomb must have thrown it over here."

The boy continued to gaze at the lake. "But it doesn't look real different at all." He sighed. "It's not like in the movies."

"No, you're right," Kady agreed, placing her arm around his shoulders. "It's not like the movies. But maybe the bomb was strong enough to kill the bad fish. I don't see it jumping."

Todd lifted his head. "You think the fish's killed dead and we can go back in the lake?"

Kady shrugged. "I don't know. But I sure hope so."

—⟋⟍—

Monique sat in her car and called Frank on her cell phone. "Hi, it's Monique," she said when he answered. "Just checking in to see what's going on."

"Good morning, Monique...Hey, you were at the lake bombing this morning. How did it go?"

"Very loud and impressive."

"No one got hurt?"

"I don't think so, unless you count a few dead fish."

"I hope one of them was our killer."

"Yeah, well, we'll have to wait and see about that...What's happening with you?"

"I still haven't been able to reach that diver to show him those pictures. Mr. Marshall hasn't spoken publicly to anyone except the police since right after the accident. He's gone somewhere to hide and I'm not going to be able to find him so we'll just have to wait until he's ready to come back."

"That injured policeman already agreed the jumping fish looks like the Coccosteus, so we do have one more witness," Monique said. "Think that's enough to convince the world that our killer is a prehistoric, extinct fish?"

Frank chuckled.

The reporter was quiet for a moment. "Any progress with linking the fish to a species that's still alive?"

"No. We still don't have a match."

"Anything else happening science-wise?"

Frank hesitated before answering. "Well, a few of the folks here have been working on something..."

"What?"

"I really can't tell you what it is. That's why I didn't mention anything earlier."

"Thanks a lot," Monique said sarcastically. "That's real helpful."

"I'm sorry, but I'm not allowed to say anything. In fact, I shouldn't be talking about it at all, even vaguely...Listen, Monique, if our mystery fish was killed by today's bomb, we won't need this. And if the bomb didn't work and the jumping fish is still alive, then you'll find out about this scientific breakthrough very soon."

"All right, I guess."

"Sorry."

"But you will call me if something happens that you *can* tell me?

Right?"

"Promise."

—⟋m⟍—

"Hey, you guys want some lunch?"

Kady and Todd, playing a game of checkers on the boy's back porch, both looked up when they heard Monique's voice.

"Have you eaten yet?" Monique continued as she reached the table.

"Uh uh." Todd shook his head, staring at the two Burger King bags the reporter carried. "What's in there?"

"Well, I didn't know exactly what you both like so I got a bunch of different stuff," Monique said as she put the bags on the table and opened them, removing the wrapped items of food and arranging each piece in a straight line. "I have Whopper Juniors, hamburgers, Chicken Tenders, and fries." She looked at Kady. "I didn't get sodas because I figured we should at least drink something healthy, like milk or juice. So if you two are hungry, we can eat right now. Then I'll tell you about my idea for this afternoon."

"I'm *really* hungry!" Todd said, rubbing his stomach. He quickly tossed the checkers and checkerboard into the box.

Kady brought out glasses and a carton of milk and they each made selections from the assortment of food.

"Yum!" Todd said, noisily chewing a Whopper Junior.

"Thanks a lot," the girl said as she reached for another Chicken Tender. "I haven't had Burger King in a while."

"I was going there anyway for lunch and coming back here, so I figured you both might enjoy it too." Monique took a sip of milk. "How did this morning go?"

"Boom!" Todd yelled, raising his arms.

Kady frowned and then shook her head at the boy.

"Well, that's what happened this morning." He took another big bite.

"We couldn't see anything, but the bomb was real loud," Kady said. "When we came back here, we looked at the lake and it seems pretty much the same. Did they kill the fish?"

"Have you seen it jump since you came back?" Monique asked.

The girl shook her head as she munched on a fry.

"Let's hope nobody sees it," Monique continued, nibbling on her hamburger.

"You mentioned something about this afternoon," Kady said.

"Yeah." The reporter lowered her burger. "It's real hot today and, of course, you can't go swimming here." She gestured at the lake. "How about we all go to the town pool?"

"Can we?" Todd asked Kady.

"I can call your mom and ask her if it's okay."

"Tell Todd's mother that one of us will always be in the water with him," Monique added. "Even if there's a lifeguard on duty, we won't leave him by himself...I'll talk to her if she has a problem."

"Okay." Kady walked inside to make the phone call.

Jill Cimino gave permission for her son to go to the pool so, after lunch, Todd quickly put on his swimming trunks and grabbed an old towel. Then he, Kady, and Monique headed next door to the Gonzalez's house. Todd waited in the living room while the females went into Kady's room to change.

"You packed a bathing suit?" Kady asked as she undressed.

"Of course." Monique stepped into the bottom of a bright yellow bikini with purple polka dots. "I told you, I'm always prepared. That's why I have so much shit." She indicated the two large suitcases and duffle bag.

The teen wriggled into her favorite swimsuit, a muted pink maillot with a small ruffled skirt. Turning to the side, she stared at her reflection in the dresser mirror and frowned. "This suit makes me look even more flat-chested."

"There you go again, puttin' yourself down." Monique walked to Kady and hugged her. "I told you, you've gotta be patient about the boobs...And meanwhile, learn to like yourself."

"Easy for you to talk." Kady pulled away and pointed to Monique's shapely body. "You look like that."

"Yeah, but I'm twenty-six and you're just thirteen. Give it..."

A loud bang on the door interrupted Monique's pep talk. "C'mon!" Todd shouted. "What's taking both of you so long? I wanna go swimming!"

"All right," Kady said. "Stop making all that noise. We're coming out."

—w—

After Monique parked the car, the three of them walked to the pool area, with Todd leading the way. "C'mon," he urged, looking over his shoulder. "You girls walk too slow."

"And you walk too fast," Monique said, smiling at the little boy's impatience.

They found a clear spot on the grass and spread their towels. Todd bounced up immediately. "Okay, I don't wanna sit," he said. "I wanna go in the water."

Kady looked at Monique. "I'll go with him," she said.

"Do you want me to go too so you can swim?" Monique asked.

The girl shook her head. "Then we have to carry all our stuff with us and there's no place to sit. We can take turns watching Todd so you stay here this time."

"Fine." Rolling onto her stomach, Monique closed her eyes. "I'm pooped so I'm not going to argue with you. If I fall asleep, just wake me up when it's my turn."

The boy scooped up his towel and rushed towards the pool as Kady tried to keep pace. "Slow down, Todd," she said. "This isn't a race."

"I wanna go swim." Throwing the towel on the concrete floor abutting the pool, he jumped into the shallow end.

After tossing her towel next to Todd's, Kady stepped gingerly into the water. "It's pretty cold," she said.

"Nah, it's fine. I'm gonna swim to the deep end."

"Wait for me." Bracing herself, Kady lowered her body into the water and swam after Todd.

"See, it's not so cold," he said when she reached him.

"It's warmer if you keep moving," she agreed, treading water.

"I'm gonna go out and jump back in." Todd climbed up the ladder and, holding his nose, jumped into the pool. When he surfaced, a huge smile covered his face. "That was so cool. Watch me do it again." He ran out of the water and repeated the jump.

"What'cha staring at, Fraidy Kady?"

Kady stiffened when she heard Hannah's voice directly behind her. Still monitoring Todd's jumps, she continued to tread water and didn't turn around.

"Who's that—your boyfriend?" Hannah teased.

"I'm babysitting him."

"Oh, that's right. I forgot. You're *really* poor. You don't have any money so you need a job."

"I *like* to babysit. It's fun."

"Well maybe you should use some of the money to buy yourself a new bathing suit. The one you're wearing really sucks. It looks like it's for a baby. Bye, Fraidy Kady Baby. Goo-goo, ga-ga!"

Hearing the sounds of giggling and splashes as Hannah swam away, Kady continued to dog paddle and watch Todd jump into the pool. She tried not to think about what Hannah had said, knowing the girl wanted to make her cry. But Kady agreed with Hannah's assessment of her bathing suit. Although it was the best one she had, it was two-years-old and barely fit. It did make her look like a little baby. She felt her eyes start to get watery.

"Todd!" she called, hoping her voice sounded normal. "That's enough jumping and swimming for now. Let's check on how Monique's doing and then you can go back in the water with her."

"Promise I can come right back?" the boy asked as he reluctantly headed for the ladder.

"Yeah. Monique will take you." Kady and Todd grabbed their towels and began walking to the grassy area.

—〰—

"Wake up! I still wanna go in the pool! I'm not done swimming!"

Monique opened her eyes at the sound of Todd's voice. "What are you two doing here so soon?"

"Kady made me come out of the water. But she promised you would take me right back."

Monique stared at the teen's unhappy face. "What the hell happened?" she asked.

"Hannah's here."

"That nasty girl?"

Kady nodded.

"Jeez!" Monique stood up and crossed her arms. "What does she look like? What's she wearing?"

"Hannah's real pretty. She's got blue eyes and long blonde hair." Kady shrugged. "But I don't know what she's wearing...I didn't see her."

"Huh?" Tilting her head, the reporter looked at Kady, dumbfounded.

"She swam up behind me and just started talking. I was watching Todd jump in the pool, so I didn't turn around."

"A real sneak attack...My toilet paper idea didn't work?"

"No."

"I guess that's not good for the pool. You have to actually see the person—and she has to be wearing regular clothes. What did Hannah say this time?"

"Oh, that I'm poor and this is a baby bathing suit." Kady touched her pink frilly skirt. "She's right. I hate this..."

Todd tugged impatiently on Monique's arm. "Stop talking about stupid clothes! C'mon! You're taking too long. Kady said I could go right back into the pool."

Monique picked up her towel and slowly began walking

backwards, the boy still pulling her arm. "We'll talk about this later tonight so don't think about her anymore. Okay?" Todd released her arm and continued heading towards the pool.

Kady shook her head. "No, I am going to think about Hannah." Reaching into her bag, she pulled out her notebook. "I can use the bad stuff she said in my story." She forced a small smile. "I'm making my 'Mean Girls' really mean."

After a quick wave, Monique turned and ran after Todd.

—m—

>   Anna spit directly in Kathy's face. *"You're so ugly, even your own mother didn't want you,"* she said.

>   Kathy used her hand to wipe off both the spit and her tears...

"Whatcha doing?" Todd dripped water on Kady's back as he peered over her shoulder. Monique stood next to him.

"I'm writing a story," the girl explained as she closed her notebook.

"Why? It's the summer. You're not in school."

Kady sat up and smiled. "Because I like to make up stuff and write it down. It's fun."

Todd wrinkled his nose and made a disapproving face. "No, it's not. Writing is stupid work." He pointed towards the pool. "Swimming is fun."

"Speaking of swimming, how about we take our things and go back to the pool one last time so Kady can go into the water again," Monique suggested.

"That's okay. I can stay here and write."

"I don't think that mean girl's there anymore. I didn't see anyone that looked like the way you described her."

Kady smiled. "Then let's go."

Picking up their bags and towels, they headed for the pool. Monique again watched Todd while Kady swam and, without Hannah teasing her, she was able to relax and enjoy the water.

—⟨⟨⟩⟩—

Later in the afternoon, Monique drove from the pool to Todd's house. Before going inside, they all walked to his backyard to again check the lake.

"It looks the same," Kady said. "Very peaceful."

"No jumping fish," Monique added.

"Look, over there!" Todd pointed to the left, where several dead fish still lay. "What's that?"

"It's just a seagull poking at the fish that were killed this morning," the reporter explained. "It's not the jumping fish." Then she turned around and headed to Kady's house.

—⟨⟨⟩⟩—

For Wednesday night's dinner, Monique took Kady and Edgar to a popular local steakhouse. They all agreed the food was excellent. "Best T-bone I've ever had," Edgar said as he lowered himself into the backseat of Monique's car. They returned to the Gonzalez's house just in time for the local TV news.

Monique sat in the loveseat and Edgar plopped his body into the upholstered chair as Kady lay on the floor and turned on the TV. After a commercial, the blond anchorman's face filled the screen. "Good evening, this is Rob Kendrick with the nightly news. As usual these days, we begin this evening with an update on the latest situation in Peachwood Lake. Here is Rachel Castell, our reporter who has been covering this story since it began. Rachel, what is going on with the killer fish?"

The scene switched to the redheaded reporter, again standing with her back facing the lake. "Good evening, Rob. I'm at Fairview Day Camp, where this morning the Air Force dropped a bomb into the middle of Peachwood Lake to kill the fish that has been terrorizing the residents of this small town. Here is what happened." A picture of an explosion in the water filled the screen.

"Wow! Monique, is that what you saw?" Kady asked.

"Yeah, but I practically had to cover my ears and my eyes because of all the noise and the blowing sand."

Rachel was again talking. "As you could see, the blast was quite powerful. Thankfully, no one was hurt and the only damage reported was two broken windows by rocks kicked up from the explosion. Now town officials are hopeful that the bomb did, in fact, kill the jumping fish. I spoke to Mayor Turnbull immediately after the blast." The picture shifted to the rumpled-looking Peachwood official, standing in front of the Fairview camp building.

"What is the town's next step?" Rachel asked.

"Well, now we just have to wait to find out if anyone sees the jumping fish again. We have set up a hotline for residents to call if they see the fish jump in Peachwood Lake. The number people should call if they see the fish is 555-FISH." The mayor paused briefly and then turned so she completely faced the TV audience. "Please call only if you see a jumping fish."

Rachel was back on camera, microphone in her hand. "The good news is that, so far, no one has called the town about the fish or used that number, which, of course, means no one has seen the fish jump today." The reporter sighed. "That's a real good sign."

"Can you please give us that phone number again, Rachel?" the anchorman asked.

"Sure, Rob. It's 555-FISH."

"Thanks, Rachel...Now turning to other news..."

Kady hit the "Mute" button on the remote. "What do you want to do tonight?" she asked.

Monique stood and smiled at the Gonzalezes. "Well, if you folks will excuse me, I'm going to check my messages. Then I have to put my brain into think-mode to come up with a new and exciting angle for tomorrow morning's *Weird World* article."

Kady also rose and faced her father. "I'm going to my room too, Dad. I want to work on my story and read what Monique wrote about the bomb today. Then maybe I can help her find an idea for her article." She kissed him lightly on his cheek and handed him the remote. "Hope you won't be too lonely."

"You girls go ahead and do your important writing," he said. "I'll be fine. I have the TV for company." Edgar changed the channels until he found a baseball game and switched on the sound. "Don't worry about me. I'll just relax here watching the Red Sox."

—⟋⟍⟍—

As soon as Kady entered the bedroom, Monique closed the door behind her. "I want to talk to you," she said.

"I thought you had to check your messages."

"I just said that so I could leave the living room and come in here. I knew you'd follow me. I already checked my phone before dinner and the only message was my office telling me that no one's seen the fish yet...If the fish's dead, they want me to do a wrap-up story and leave Peachwood Lake."

"Oh." Kady lowered herself onto her bed. "When would you go?"

"Sometime late tomorrow."

Kady frowned. Monique sat next to her and put her arms around the girl. "Listen, that doesn't mean I'll never see you again. We'll call each other all the time and I'll come to visit."

"I know, but..."

"But what?"

"It's been so great having you here."

Monique freed herself and stood up. "Listen, girl. We gotta talk." Placing her hands on her slim hips, she shook her head, jingling her hoop earrings. "No more of this 'Poor Me' bullshit. You got to get your act together." After dragging the desk chair next to Kady's bed, she sat in it and leaned forward. "Now I want to hear about the clothes."

"What about the clothes?"

"Let's start with the bathing suit problem."

Kady stared at her hands. "I hate all my bathing suits. Hannah was right. They're old and they make me look like a baby."

"Would you let me buy you a couple of new ones?"

"No. My dad would be mad."

"Can you buy them yourself using your babysitting money?"

"Todd's mom hasn't paid me yet."

"How about a loan then? You can pay me back when you get the money."

Kady looked up and smiled. "That could work."

The reporter jumped up. "Fine. Tomorrow, after dinner—before I go home—you and I will go shopping. This time of the season all the bathing suits will be on sale so maybe we'll pick out a few other things too."

Monique moved to the desk, opened her laptop, and gestured to Kady. "Go ahead and read my last article. Then I've gotta rack my brain to think of a new angle for tomorrow's fish story. I wasn't lying about that part."

CHAPTER 17

"Let's go down to the lake," Mike McConnelly said. Without waiting for a reaction to his words, he turned off the TV and stood up. At six-foot-five, with a burly frame and bushy black hair and beard, the college senior was an imposing figure.

He looks just like Moses, Connor Dobkins thought, gazing up at the man from the floor of the frat house. The slightly-built high school graduate checked his watch. "But it's really late, Mike...After two in the morning. Can't we just go to sleep?" He faked a yawn, dramatically stretching his arms.

"No," Mike said. "In fact, right now's the perfect time." He walked to the couch, where a lanky young man with tousled long blond hair and a small tuft of hair on his chin snored softly. "Ken, wake up!" Mike demanded, shaking him roughly. "I need you to get the hell up now!"

"Huh?" Ken Saviola opened his eyes and glared at Mike. "What's f___in' goin' on?"

"We're heading over to the lake," Mike said. "Splash some water on your face and then we're leaving."

"Shit," Ken muttered as he stumbled towards the bathroom. "I was havin' a great dream about me and Amy."

—◌◌◌—

Early Thursday morning, Mike drove his battered Volkswagen to Peachwood Lake, making the five-mile trip in less than ten minutes, and parked in the small lot adjoining the town's meager property. The public lakefront consisted of two picnic tables, a men's and women's one-stall bathroom, a water fountain, and a tiny roped-off swimming area.

The restrooms had long been a hangout for vagrants and drug users so town residents had avoided the site completely. However, in the spring, Mayor Turnbull's administration had cleaned up the property and now a few mothers brought their young children to the area, especially during swimming season. But, despite the mayor's efforts, the public recreation site still remained mostly unused.

Mike and Ken walked past the bathrooms, a dim bare bulb providing a small amount of light, and sat next to each other at one of the picnic tables.

Connor followed and took a seat opposite them. "Why are we here?" he asked.

Mike looked at Ken and smiled. "We thought it would be a good night for a swim," he said.

Connor stared at the large bearded man. "Are you f___in' psycho?" he asked. "Didn't you hear about the jumping fish that's been killing people?" He pointed to a pole next to the lake. "There's even signs all over telling you not to go into the water."

"Didn't you hear about the bomb?" Mike rose to his feet and leaned his massive body towards Connor. "They f___in' blew up the whole lake. The goddamn fish is dead. I heard on TV that no one's seen it since yesterday morning."

Holy shit! Realizing Mike was serious, Connor backed away from the big man.

"Yeah," Ken said. "What the hell. A little nighttime swim would be good."

"Remember what I said about pledging Zeta Alpha Nu?" Mike asked, sitting down again. "You're gonna have to do lots of shit like this. We need to find out if you got the balls to be a ZAN."

Until last night, Connor hadn't even thought about pledging a fraternity. But he had started talking to some ZAN guys on campus and then gone with them to the frat party. After drinking too much, he didn't want to drive home so Mike had invited him to sleep over. And now this was happening.

"But pledging's not for a few weeks—after school starts," Connor finally said.

"Yeah," the big man agreed. "But we're not too sure about you so you need to do a little pre-pledging before we decide if we're even gonna let you into the pledge class." He smiled at Ken and then headed to the edge of the lake with his fellow frat member following. Turning around, he grinned at Connor, who still sat at the picnic table. "So? You coming?"

Connor slid off the bench and slowly began walking towards Peachwood Lake.

Mike took off his sneakers and socks and dipped one foot into the lake. "Feels good, nice and warm," he said, nudging Connor. "Go ahead. Take off your shoes and try it."

The high school graduate followed Mike's instructions and cautiously stepped into the water.

"How is it?" the big man asked.

"Okay, I guess," Connor said, moving back to the shore.

"Now take off your shirt and jeans," Mike commanded.

Connor hesitated.

"You gonna f___in' do this or not?" Ken asked angrily.

"But I'm not wearing a suit."

"So what?" Mike said. "You can swim in your underwear. No one'll see you and then you'll dry off."

"What if the fish's still alive?"

"It's not," Mike said. "You're only gonna swim a little anyway and this is a f___in' baby pool." He pointed to the small roped-off area, which was about twenty feet long. "That fish hung out just in the middle of the lake, in the deep water."

Connor spread out his hands, palms up. "What do I have to do?"

"You swim five laps back and forth, for a total of ten," Mike said. "Whole thing should take you about three minutes max."

"If I do that, then you'll let me pledge ZAN?"

"Yeah, sure," Ken said, turning to Mike. "Right?"

The big man nodded his head.

"Okay then." Connor quickly pulled off his tee shirt and jeans. "Here goes." Taking a deep breath, he cautiously entered the water.

—ɯ—

"What was that?" Connor asked. Standing in water up to his waist, he stopped moving and called to the shore. "Something just touched my leg. I thought you said they bombed the lake and there was no fish here anymore."

"They bombed the *middle* of the lake," Mike said. "They just wanted to kill the one motherf___in' fish and not hurt all the others."

"Oh." Lowering himself into the water, Connor started doing his laps. Not a great swimmer and still a little drunk, he tried to move as quickly as possible.

"That's two," Mike called. "Keep going."

Connor swam another two laps, his arms feeling very tired.

"Only one more to go," Ken said. "You can do it!"

Breathing heavily, Connor labored to the rope in the deeper water and held on, trying to muster the strength to swim back to the shore. Suddenly, he heard a splash directly behind him and turned around. "Whaa...?" Before he could finish saying the word, a silver fish, flashing an open mouth filled with enormous serrated teeth, lunged at him. The armored creature latched onto Connor's neck and held on tightly.

"Help!" Connor shouted as loud as he could as he tried to keep himself afloat and pull the gnawing fish off his neck. As a result, his cry sounded more like a whispery gurgle.

"What's going on out there?" Ken asked, stepping closer to the lake. "Why isn't he swimming back?"

"I don't know," Mike said. "I thought he said something, but I couldn't understand it." The big man waded into the water up to his ankles. "Connor?" he called. "Are you okay?"

There was no response.

"He ain't answering," Mike continued. "I hear lots of splashing, but that's all and I can't see nothing. Maybe he got a cramp or something. I gotta get him the f___ out of there." Still wearing his clothes, he dove into the water and swam towards the splashing noises.

"Connor?" Mike hollered as he reached the part of the rope where the water was still swirling. He looked around, but didn't see anything. Then he felt something heavy bounce against his stomach. He reached into the water and groped for the object, which felt round and oddly familiar. Lifting it up, he found himself staring into Connor's startled blue eyes. "Shit!" He threw the decapitated head back into the lake and, swimming as fast as he could, headed towards the shore. Behind him, Mike heard a splash and, immediately afterwards, felt a sharp, piercing pain in his chest. "No-o-o-o!" he yelled.

"Mike?" Ken called. "Why'd you scream? What the f___'s happening?" He reached for his cell phone. "Shit. I'm not going in there," he muttered as he dialed 911.

CHAPTER 18

The insistent ringing of a nearby phone woke Kady out of a deep sleep. "What time is it?" she mumbled, rubbing her eyes.

"Middle of the night," Monique said as she dug inside her oversized bag and grabbed her cell phone. "Yes?" She listened quietly for a minute. "Hold on a sec, okay? I'm gonna go outside to talk." Covering the phone with her hand, she turned to Kady. "Go back to sleep and I'll tell you what's going on in the morning."

After quickly stepping into a pair of jeans and still wearing her nighttime tee shirt, the reporter dashed out the front door of the cottage. Two minutes later, she returned and began gathering her things, trying to make as little noise as possible.

"You can't see in the dark," Kady said, jumping out of bed and switching on the overhead light.

"I was doing just fine. You're supposed to be sleeping."

"I couldn't fall asleep without knowing what that call was about." The girl sat up and folded her arms. "So...?"

"So the fish may not be dead." Monique pulled off the tee and put on her bra and a short-sleeve navy top, tucking the shirt into her jeans. "That was Debbie. She said someone just called the police to report a problem in the lake. Seems some asshole went swimming in the town's rec area and something happened."

Kady stared open-mouthed at Monique. "What happened?"

"I don't know yet, but I'm going down there right now to find..."

"Please let me go with you."

The reporter shook her head emphatically. "No way, girl. Promise I'll tell you everything when I get back."

"Then I'm going to watch from the window. I'll write down what I see and maybe you can use something in your story."

"I'd rather you went to sleep, but I don't have time to argue." Monique grabbed her bag and waved. "Gotta run."

Two police cars and an old Volkswagen were the only vehicles parked in the small lot next to the town's lakefront when Monique arrived. *No media folks here yet?* she wondered as she walked past the bathrooms towards the water. *Not even the great Rachel Castell.* She chuckled softly.

When Monique reached the shoreline, now illuminated by several lanterns, she immediately stopped smiling. "What the hell happened?" she asked the nearest policeman as she stared at the two mutilated male bodies lying on the grass. She showed the officer her press ID and Pete Malone smiled. "I remember seeing you here earlier in the week," he said, gazing at her with penetrating hazel eyes.

"Because I'm black?"

"Because you're real pretty."

"Oh." Unable to come up with a clever retort, Monique took her notebook from her bag and fumbled through it for a pen. When she had regained her composure, she faced the officer again. "So how'd all this shit go down?"

"It must've been the same jumping fish," Pete said. "But our only witness didn't see anything." He pointed to the young man sitting with two other policemen, sobbing, and holding his head in his hands. "Poor kid's in shock."

"Did he tell you anything about what happened?"

"Only that he and the big bearded guy heard splashing and called to the kid who was swimming in the water. When they didn't get any response, the big man went in." Pete shrugged. "And this is what happened."

"Why did the first one go into the lake?"

"It was some kind of fraternity pledging deal. The kid, Connor was his name, wanted to join their frat and they were pulling his chain. Told him he had to swim back and forth a few times before he could even pledge."

"Didn't he know about the fish?"

"They were sure the bomb killed it."

"Oh shit." Monique lowered herself slowly onto the grass, shaking her head. "I don't believe this." Hearing loud voices, she looked up just as Rachel Castell, followed by her cameraman, came running towards them.

"Officer, what's going on here?" Rachel asked, gasping for breath.

While Pete Malone answered the TV reporter's barrage of questions, Monique found her camera and photographed the two mutilated corpses. *Gross,* she thought. *But our wacko readers will love it.*

—⚶—

Sitting in her desk chair, Kady held a pad and pencil and stared through her bedroom window, straining her eyes to see what was happening on the other side of Peachwood Lake. On the far left, she could make out some activity—lights on the shore and moving figures—but nothing else. "This isn't working," she mumbled.

The girl crept into the living room and switched on the television, quickly lowering the volume so she wouldn't disturb her father, who was asleep in the other bedroom. Flipping the stations, she saw a familiar sight—reporter Rachel Castell, standing with her microphone, in front of the lake. The graphic on the top right of the screen read "LIVE: SPECIAL REPORT." Kady turned up the sound slightly and lay on the carpet.

"...dead men have been identified as Mike McConnelly, a student at North Connecticut College and Connor Dobkins, who had just graduated from Redcrest High School in June and would have been a freshman next month at the same college."

The TV screen showed two bodies, both covered in sheets. Then the picture shifted to a close-up of Rachel, wearing less makeup than usual, but her wavy red hair looking as neat as always. The newscaster paused, shaking her head sadly. "This is truly a grisly sight. One young man with his entire chest cut open; the other man decapitated..."

Kady put her hand to her mouth. *Decapitated*...That meant his head was cut off! She tried to ignore the gruesome image of a head being chopped off by a guillotine so she could concentrate on the news bulletin.

As Rachel continued describing what had happened, the newscaster heard sounds in the background and turned her head. "Mayor Turnbull has just arrived," she announced, walking to the mayor, who was surrounded by several members of the media. "Let's hear what she has to say."

"Wow, there's Monique!" Kady murmured.

Rachel shoved her microphone in front of the mayor's face. "Mayor Turnbull, please tell us what you plan to do now."

The mayor, wearing a tight pink blouse, sighed and shook her head sadly. "This is yet another terrible tragedy," she began. "Two young men who should have had many more years. My heart goes out to their families..." She stared directly into the camera before continuing. "I want to tell you that the Town Board and I have prepared for the possibility that the fish could still be alive and I will make an announcement at nine o'clock this morning. But I want all the citizens of Peachwood to know that we will win this battle and reclaim our lake."

"Thank you, Mayor Turnbull." Rachel faced the screen again. "You heard it here. The mayor will have a statement later this morning concerning this ongoing crisis and I will be at Town Hall to report it.

This is Rachel Castell, reporting live at Peachwood Lake for WBTR News. Good night."

Kady turned off the TV and tiptoed into her bedroom.

—ɯ—

As Rachel ended her report, Monique dashed over to Pete Malone and confirmed the names and ages of the victims and the witness. "Now I've gotta go write my story," she said, closing her notebook. "But the library's not open yet and I need a place with an Internet feed. Any suggestions?"

He gave her a puzzled look.

"I'm staying with a young teen who lives on the lake with her dad and they aren't online," she explained.

"Not Kady Gonzalez?"

"Yes." She stared at the officer. "You know her?"

"Kady's the one that saw the fish kill Martin Urloch. I was there with her when they pulled him out of the water." He shook his head. "Like tonight, a tough thing for anyone to witness. Tell Kady 'hi' from me. She's a good kid."

"She sure is," Monique agreed. "Staying with Kady right on the lake helped me get here real fast. But what's the good of being here early if I have to wait till the library opens to first send my story?"

Pete grinned. "I've got the solution," he said. "You can go to the station. We've got Internet hookup."

"They'll let me sit there and write?"

"Yeah." He reached into his pocket and removed a business card from his wallet. "And if anyone gives you a problem, tell them Pete Malone told you it was okay. I'll write something on this for you. What's your name?"

"Monique Atchison."

Pete scribbled a few words on the back of the card. "Here, Monique. Now you're all set." He handed her the card.

"Thanks a lot, Pete." She smiled as she took it. Then she waved her forefinger. "Wait a minute. Your name is Pete Malone? Weren't you one of the cops out on the lake last week, trying to catch the fish?"

"Yeah, unfortunately."

"What did it look like?"

"Big mother, with tough skin that looked and felt like armor. I tried to bash it in the head, but that didn't work...Mean s.o.b."

"Hope the town can figure out a way to kill it," Monique called as she rushed towards her car. "Gotta run—and thanks again."

CHAPTER 19

MYSTERY FISH SURVIVES BOMB—
MUTILATES AND KILLS
TWO COLLEGE STUDENTS!

by Monique Atchison

PEACHWOOD, CONNECTICUT — Even a bomb couldn't destroy the monstrous creature that has been terrorizing Peachwood Lake. At about 3 a.m. Thursday morning, the razor-toothed jumping fish attacked two young men, biting them both to death.

Here's what happened: Zeta Alpha Nu president Michael McConnelly, 22, had ordered 18-year-old Connor Dobkins to swim several laps in Peachwood Lake as a pre-pledge test for joining the North Connecticut College fraternity, according to fellow ZAN member, Ken Saviola, 21, the only survivor.

When he and McConnelly heard splashing noises and Dobkins didn't respond to their calls, the frat president dove into the water to rescue him.

In a vicious attack that lasted less than five minutes, the fierce creature killed both victims, hideously mutilating them. McConnelly's entire chest was sliced open with deep zigzag cuts down the middle that look like the ghoulish handiwork of a sadistic surgeon. [Insert photo 1] But what the fish did to Dobkins is even more repulsive. [Insert photo 2] Using its unbelievably sharp teeth, the monster bit off the teen's head, which is still lying somewhere on the bottom of Peachwood Lake. Police say no one is going to look for it right now because entering the lake is just too dangerous. Only Dobkins' headless torso was retrieved.

What's the town's next step for destroying the murderous fish, which...

After mentioning that Mayor Turnbull would be making an announcement in the morning and reviewing the previous deaths, Monique emailed her story to Debbie, attaching her gruesome photos of the two dead bodies. Then she turned off her laptop, thanked the officer on duty for allowing her to work at the empty police station—she hadn't even had to show him Pete's card—and walked to her car.

Monique unlocked the front door of the Gonzalez's house and stepped inside, trying to make as little noise as possible. Taking off her sneakers, she tiptoed into Kady's bedroom and began undressing in the dark.

"The fish really messed up those two college guys, huh?" the girl asked.

"Why're you still awake?"

"It was impossible going back to sleep after hearing all that gross stuff about a chopped-off head."

"You listened to the radio?" Monique climbed into bed and picked up her alarm clock.

"No, it was on TV. Rachel Castell was at the lake and she talked about what happened. They didn't show the bodies though." Kady sat up. "I saw you there too."

"Oh...Did I look okay?"

"You looked great...Monique, I pretty much know what the fish did, but can I please read your story?"

"Now? I need to get some sleep. I just set the alarm for seven-forty-five 'cause I gotta get up early to hear the mayor."

"Ple-e-e-ase. There's never any time when we wake up."

The reporter reached for her laptop. Then she carried it carefully to the desk and switched on the lamp. "You've got five minutes. Go."

Kady jumped out of bed, rushed to the desk, and began reading. "You did a good job describing those dead bodies," she said when she had finished. "They must've been awful to look at...Can I see the photos you took?"

"No, you certainly cannot."

Frowning, the girl turned off the computer, shut the light, and returned to her bed.

"Oh, I almost forgot," Monique said. "I met someone you know and he said to say 'hi' to you."

"Who?"

"A policeman...Pete Malone."

"Yeah, he's real nice. When Mr. Urloch got killed, he was here and was worried about me and gave me his card."

"Pete gave me his card too," Monique said, fluffing her pillow. "Okay, that's enough conversation for the middle of the night. I've got less than three hours till my alarm goes off. We'll talk more tomorrow. Now go to sleep."

"I'll try, but those bodies..."

"Don't think about them anymore. Force yourself to think of something good."

Kady turned onto her stomach and thought about being a famous writer. She was at a bookstore where a long line of people waited for her to autograph copies of her best-selling novel, *Mean Girls*.

—m—

Just before nine o'clock Thursday morning, Monique stood inside Town Hall with about twenty other members of the media, waiting for Mayor Turnbull to make her announcement. She entertained herself by watching Rachel Castell give orders to her cameraman, who nodded continuously to the newscaster's commands. *The return of bobblehead man*.

Then the mayor entered the room, stepped to the podium, and placed a sheet of paper on the lectern. The audience quieted immediately.

"Good morning," Mayor Turnbull began. "This will be brief and I'm not going to answer any questions after my statement. As you all know, despite yesterday's bomb, the killer fish is still alive in Peachwood Lake. Early this morning, it murdered two young men." She removed her glasses and wiped her eyes with her left hand. "First, I would like to send my sincere condolences to the families of Connor Dobkins and Michael McConnelly for their terrible losses. I really hope this is the last time I will be up here talking about deaths in Peachwood Lake."

After putting her glasses back on, the mayor glanced at the sheet of paper. "This is what we are going to do now. Our scientists at Connecticut State Labs have developed a liquid poison that they believe will kill this particular fish."

People in the audience began mumbling to one another.

"Hold on," Mayor Turnbull said, raising her left hand and looking up. "I know what you're thinking because I asked the scientists the same question: How can they develop a poison when they don't even know what kind of fish this is? Here's what they told me." She scanned the paper. "They've adapted an existing natural toxin to create a new formula they call Nervirula. It's specifically aimed to kill just bony-plated fish, which we know this creature is. They assure me it won't hurt people or affect the water and it shouldn't harm any other types of fish, nor crustaceans, and it won't damage the sea plants, which should ease the fears of members of the Ecological Protection Patrol."

She folded the paper and stared at the media representatives. "An Air Force plane is going to dump this poison into the lake at two o'clock this afternoon. Since the fish isn't just swimming in the center anymore, they're going to drop poison in five parts of the lake to be sure all of the water is affected. If this plan is successful, we'll know almost immediately. The poison should kill the fish within minutes." She smiled weakly at the crowd of reporters. "I don't have any more details, so I'm not fielding questions. That's it for now. Thank you all for coming...Keep your fingers crossed and wish us luck."

—∽∾∽—

"...and that wraps up this morning's announcement from Town Hall. This is Rachel Castell, reporting live for WBTR-TV."

Kady turned off the Cimino's television and turned to Todd. "Okay, so now that we know what they're going to do to the lake, what do you want to do this morning?"

"I wanna see the plane drop the poison."

"It's not going to be exciting, like the bomb," Kady explained. "They're just dumping stuff into the lake this time so there's nothing to see."

"But then the bad fish'll be killed dead. We'll see it jump up and fall over like this." After leaping as high as he could, Todd fell onto the living room floor, face up, with his arms and legs spread-eagled. Then he closed his eyes and pretended to gurgle water.

Kady smiled. "You make a great dead fish, Todd. Maybe you can get on TV with your act."

"You really think so?" the boy asked, sitting up. "That'd be real cool and I'll have lots and lots of money."

"Yeah, sounds like a good career for you—professional dead fish impersonator." She giggled. "But that's in the future. What do you want to do now? The plane's not dropping the poison in the lake till the afternoon."

"Let's play cards...How about war?" Todd dashed into his room.

The reporters walked out of Town Hall grumbling about the mayor's statement. "Just what the hell is this Nervirula shit?" the man behind Monique asked.

"The mayor said it's something new," a woman replied.

"Now I gotta call Connecticut State Labs and find some damn scientist who's willing to talk to me," the man continued. "That could take all morning."

Monique smiled and continued to her car. Once inside the Elantra, she took out her cell phone and dialed a number.

"Hello," a male voice said.

"Hi, Frank. It's Monique. I've just come from the mayor's press conference at Town Hall. Is this what you couldn't talk to me about yesterday?"

"The Nervirula announcement? Now you see why I couldn't discuss it, even off the record." The scientist sighed. "I was really hoping it wouldn't be necessary."

"Can you give me a little more information on Nervirula?" Monique asked as she flipped her notebook to a blank page. "Exactly what is it?"

After listening to Frank's explanation and taking notes, Monique thanked him and headed to the library to write her story.

CHAPTER 20

TOWN POISONING KILLER FISH TODAY!
by Monique Atchison

PEACHWOOD, CONNECTICUT — Germ warfare. That's the next weapon this embattled small town will hurl at the murderous creature that's taken full control of its lake.

At 2 p.m. today (Thursday), an Air Force plane will drop Nervirula, a newly-developed liquid poison, into Peachwood Lake, hoping the toxin will kill the mysterious jumping fish. Peachwood Mayor Margaret Turnbull announced the plan at a brief morning press conference.

What is Nervirula? The mayor didn't provide any details except that the poison was created by Connecticut State Labs to kill just bony-plated fish.

A scientific expert close to the case gave *Weird World Weekly* more information, explaining

Nervirula was adapted from an existing natural toxin formed by a microscopic alga, called *Karenia brevis,* that affects the central nervous system of fish. A concentration of these algae can produce a "red tide," which paralyzes numerous sea creatures so they can't breathe.

Nervirula, a new strain of this alga, is supposed to affect just one type of fish: the armored killer in Peachwood Lake. According to scientists, the new poison won't harm people or any other aquatic life forms. If this plan works, the killer fish should die almost instantly. The fish has already been responsible for the deaths of six people...

After another brief recap of all the lake victims, Monique emailed her article, along with a photo of a red tide on the Gulf Coast she had found on the Internet, to Debbie. Then she turned off her computer and left the library.

"Hi, Kady," a male voice said. "Is everything okay?"

Kady, who was sitting in the grass next to Todd in the boy's backyard Thursday afternoon, glanced up and saw Officer Pete Malone grinning at her. She lowered the glittering mica rock the two of them had been examining and gave the policeman a perplexed look. "I'm okay. Are you here because something's wrong again?"

Pete chuckled. "No, I'm just making my rounds along the lake and I thought I'd stop by and say hello. Hope I didn't scare you."

"You didn't scare *me*," Todd said. "Nothin' scares me."

Kady rolled her eyes at the boy.

"Well, maybe the jumping fish scares me just a little," he admitted and turned to Pete. "We're gonna watch them poison it later."

"Me too," the officer said, nodding his head. "Hope the poison works." He scanned the yard. "Is your friend, Monique, here? I thought I'd check on how she was doing after last night. Did she tell you I saw her at the lake?"

"Yes, when she came in, real late...But Monique went to Town Hall this morning and she's not back yet."

"I just wanted to know if she was able to write her story okay. She needed a place hooked up to the Internet and I told her to go to the police station."

"Well, I know that Monique wrote the article because I made her let me read it," Kady said. "So I guess she didn't have a problem... Monique didn't say what time she'd be back. Sometimes she stays in town to do other stuff and doesn't come here till dinner time."

"That's okay," Pete said. He took a few steps towards the street before turning towards Kady and Todd again. "Just tell her I came by to say hello." Then he continued walking to his patrol car.

—ɯ—

"How's it going?" Kady and Todd were in Todd's backyard playing catch when Monique approached them.

"Officer Malone came here looking for you over an hour ago," Kady said. Holding the ball, she walked next to Monique and smiled. "I think he likes you."

"I don't know..." The reporter dropped onto the lawn and pulled out a piece of grass, which she began to carefully examine.

Todd ran to the girl and yanked her arm. "C'mon! Stop talking about all that stupid mushy stuff! We're right in the middle of a game!"

"Give me a minute," Kady said, pushing the boy away. "This is important. What happened at the meeting?"

"The town's going to poison the lake." Monique crumpled the blade of grass.

"Yeah, we heard that on TV. But won't it kill all the fish and hurt the water?"

"The mayor said it's supposed to just kill the armored fish and not hurt people or damage anything else in the lake," Monique said.

"Then I called Frank and he agreed that it should be safe. She glanced at her watch. "It's not two o'clock yet so there's still time." Smiling at Todd who was frowning at both of them, she bounced up and ran several yards away. "How about if I play too? Throw me the ball, Kady!"

—◯◯—

When they heard the sound of an approaching plane a few minutes later, Kady, Todd, and Monique immediately stopped their game of catch. Rushing to the edge of the lake, they sat on the grass and Monique grabbed her camera.

"I never saw poison before," Todd said. "What's it look like?"

"There are all different types," Monique explained. "This is special poison, a liquid they're pouring into the lake, that's supposed to just kill the jumping fish."

"How do they know that?" he asked.

"They're scientists," Kady said. "They're very smart people."

"We hope," the reporter whispered.

As the three of them watched, the V-22 Osprey hovered overhead, slowing to a near stop.

"It's that funny-looking plane again," Todd said. He stood up and did his imitation of a whirling helicopter.

"I know," Monique agreed. "It's a new kind of plane that can take off and land like a helicopter, but flies like a plane. That must be why the Air Force is using it."

"Well it's still goofy looking."

"Look, Todd." Kady grabbed the boy's arm and pointed to the plane. "See what it's doing now?"

The tilt-rotor plane released a small amount of liquid to their right. Then it veered left, hovered, and dropped another dose. The V-22 Osprey dumped three more loads of liquid in scattered parts of the lake before quickly flying away. Monique snapped several photos, trying to capture the plane dropping the poison.

"What's gonna happen now?" Todd asked Monique.

"We watch the lake and look for a dead fish."

"But there are still dead fish around from the bomb," he said.

"Yeah, but those have all been chewed," Kady pointed out. "They look real gross."

"And the jumping fish is plated," Monique added. "It looks different. Kady saw it and said the fish looks like it's wearing armor so we'll recognize it if it's floating on top of the water."

They watched the lake carefully.

"What's that?" the boy asked. He stood and pointed straight ahead to a round, dark green object floating motionless in the lake.

"It looks like a turtle shell," Kady said, standing.

Monique joined them. "You're right," she agreed. "It's a turtle." She sat down again and pounded her fist in the ground. "Shit!"

"There's another one!" Todd pointed to his left.

"What's going on?" Kady asked Monique, sitting next to her.

"Turtles have bony shells so I think this new poison is killing them. If that's the case, it'll probably affect all the shelled animals in the lake."

"What about the killer fish?" Kady continued.

"We'll just have to wait and see."

—⚏—

Ten minutes later, Kady, Monique, and Todd still hadn't seen the jumping fish. But the lake's surface was littered with the bodies of turtles, crayfish, and other small bony-shelled creatures.

The reporter photographed the sad scene. Then she shook her head in disgust. "That's it, folks. The show's over. Lots of dead animals, but no dead killer fish."

Kady turned to face Monique. "Maybe it just takes longer for the poison to work on the fish," she suggested.

"I don't think so." Monique stashed the camera in her big bag and began walking towards Kady's cottage. "I'm gonna head back to the library and write my story."

"I see it!" Todd screamed. "The bad fish! Over there!"

Monique rushed back to the edge of the lake. "Where?" she

asked, groping in her bag for her camera. "Does it look like it's dying?"

"No, it's jumping!" He waved his arm towards the left. "See?"

"Damn!" the reporter said as she followed Todd's gestures. "The poison didn't work at all. Goddamn fish looks healthy and strong." She zoomed in on the creature and snapped several pictures.

"I think it's eating one of the dead animals," Todd said. "The fish's stopped jumping around, but the water's moving right where it was." The boy gnashed his teeth and made loud chomping noises.

"You're probably right," Kady said, staring at the water. Then she turned to Monique. "Should we call the special number that was on TV to tell them the fish is still alive?"

"I guess so." Monique again tossed the camera into her bag and took out her cell phone. "It's 555-FISH, right?"

The girl nodded.

Monique dialed the number and spoke. "Hello. I want to report seeing the killer fish jumping in Peachwood Lake." She listened for a moment. "Oh, I see. Okay. Bye."

"What'd they say?" Kady asked.

"The woman on the phone said she'd already had about twenty calls from people who saw the fish."

"So what happens next?" Kady asked.

Monique shrugged her shoulders. "I have no idea."

CHAPTER 21

KILLER FISH STILL ALIVE!

by Monique Atchison

PEACHWOOD, CONNECTICUT — Not even poison could kill it. The mysterious jumping fish continues its siege of Peachwood Lake, where it has already murdered six people.

On Thursday afternoon, an Air Force plane dumped a newly-created poison, called Nervirula, into the crystal-clear lake. The toxin was designed specifically to kill only the bony-plated fish. Sadly, Nervirula destroyed other shelled animals, including turtles and crayfish, many of which now float lifelessly on the water's surface. The armored fish? It was seen vigorously jumping in the lake soon after the poison was dropped.

The war against the mysterious creature began when Martin Urloch...

Monique again recounted all the gruesome deaths in Peachwood Lake. "No such thing as too much gore for *Weird World*," she muttered. After emailing her photo of the killer fish jumping amidst the floating turtle bodies, she sent the article to her editor.

Just as Monique was leaving the library's parking lot Thursday afternoon, her cell phone rang. After stopping the Elantra, she greeted the caller and listened briefly.

"Okay, Debbie, I will," she said. "Glad you liked the story and thanks for the update." Then she dropped the phone into her bag and drove to Kady's house.

—◆—

Todd saw the reporter approaching as he kicked the soccer ball to Kady. "Hi, Monique," he said, running towards her.

"You finished your story?" Kady asked as she picked up the ball.

"Yeah. I'm done." Monique lowered herself onto the grass. "My editor just called to tell me the mayor's making a statement on TV at five-thirty."

"Any idea what she's going to say?" Kady asked as she sat next to Monique and let go of the ball. Todd grabbed it and continued to play a solo game of soccer around the backyard.

"Of course, it'll be about what the town's gonna do next to kill the fish." Monique shrugged. "But I sure as hell haven't a clue about what that plan is."

"What else can they do? Nothing seems to work."

"That's for sure...We'll watch tonight, before we go to dinner. Then, remember, we've got a shopping date to get you some new clothes." Monique pointed her forefinger at Kady.

"I didn't forget."

"Good."

"But not too many...I'm going to pay you back with my babysitting money."

"I know. It's not charity, just a loan."

"Right." Kady nodded her head.

—m—

Kady, Monique, and Edgar sat in the Gonzalez's living room discussing the day's events. After peeking at her watch, the reporter took out a pad and pen. "Please turn on the TV," she said to Kady. "It's almost time for the mayor's announcement."

"What do you think she'll do now?" Edgar asked Monique.

"Kady and I talked about it earlier and we've got no clue." As she gazed at the television, the commercial ended. "Here's the mayor. Let's watch."

Mayor Turnbull, wearing a tight black pantsuit, stood at the Town Hall podium looking very serious as she faced the camera. "Good evening," she began. "This afternoon, we used a new poison to try to destroy the murderous fish that has been killing people in Peachwood Lake." She took off her glasses and sighed. "Unfortunately, that plan didn't work. Many of you called to tell us that, right after the poison was dropped into the lake, you saw the fish jumping around."

The mayor put her glasses back on. "As you probably know by now, the poison did kill numerous turtles and other shelled creatures in the lake. As an animal lover, I am deeply saddened by what happened and I apologize to all the other animal lovers out there." She shook her head. "Please understand. Nervirula was so new—our scientists thought it was a miraculous breakthrough—and we were so desperate to get rid of the fish that we didn't test the toxin as thoroughly as we usually do." She sighed again. "We just wanted to save the lake. Unfortunately, that's no longer going to be possible."

Mayor Turnbull took a sheet of paper from her pants pocket and glanced at it. "If you recall, when I was talking about possible methods for destroying the jumping fish, I mentioned 'drastic options.' Now, since nothing we tried has worked, we must move forward in that direction." She again shook her head sadly. "We cannot allow this dangerous situation to continue any longer. Even though we have signs posted all along the lake warning everyone not to go into the water, some people have disobeyed the signs and three of them have been killed. We can't do anything else to protect our citizens. It's not like we can fence off the entire lake—and what good would that do anyway? Some people would just climb over it."

After a pause, the mayor continued. "So here is what we are going to do. On Saturday morning, we will begin dredging Peachwood Lake. Because of the dangerous situation here, we have gotten emergency permits from the government so we can get this procedure done as quickly as possible. We've already had experts working out the details, including a pipeline that will carry the sediment to a disposal area. They're not sure yet how long this whole process will take, but they'll start by emptying all the water."

The mayor stared directly at the TV audience. "I am so sorry to have to do this. It means all the animals living in the lake will be destroyed. It means all the aquatic plants will die too. It means the businesses that rely on the lake for their income will be devastated. And, of course, it also means no beautiful lake for boating or swimming for at least the rest of this season for all Peachwood residents."

Mayor Turnbull pushed her glasses closer to the bridge of her nose. "But, at this time, the Town Board was left with no other choice. We can no longer endanger the lives of our citizens. So, with a heavy heart, I must apologize to all of you for taking this extreme action. Please forgive me, but understand that we have just run out of choices. The one thing we can be sure of now is that when the dredging process is completed, at least the monstrous killer fish will be dead." She sighed. "Thank you for your understanding and good night."

"Wow!" Kady said, turning around. "No more lake!"

"Ssh." Edgar pointed to the television. "They're still talking."

"...you have it," the blond anchorman said. "On Saturday, the town of Peachwood will start draining its beautiful lake." He turned to the young woman sitting next to him. "Rachel Castell, you've been covering this fish story from the beginning. What do you think about this decision?"

The redheaded reporter scowled and shook her head angrily. "It's awful, Rob. There must have been something else the town could have done instead of resorting to this stupid move. It'll ruin everything!" Rachel stood up, grabbed some papers on the desk, and marched out of camera range.

"Thank you for watching this special news report," the anchorman said, glancing perplexedly at Rachel's vacant seat. "We now return to..."

"Wow!" Monique said. "A hissy fit on TV news...Don't see that too often."

"Well, I agree with her," Kady said, switching off the television. "I can see why she's so upset because the whole thing just sounds so awful. They're going to drain all the water out of the lake?"

"Yeah, they are." Monique nodded. "Guess that's the end of both the fish and my stories about it. Not a real exciting finish." She put her notebook and pen in her oversized bag.

"Will they be able to find out what kind of fish it is?" Edgar asked.

"Maybe," Monique said. "But they'd have to examine every fish that comes through their pipe. It's possible, but who the hell knows." She shrugged her shoulders. "Come on. Let's go eat dinner." She looked at Edgar. "If it's okay with you, Kady and I are going shopping for clothes afterwards."

"I'm using my babysitting money, Dad," Kady explained. "Monique's going to help me find some good stuff—bathing suits and a few other things."

"That's fine." Turning towards Monique, he spread his hands and shook his head. "I don't know much about girl's clothing."

The reporter smiled. "Most men don't...So where do you two want to eat?" Her cell phone rang and she picked it up, checking the number. "It's my editor," she said. "Excuse me." Opening the phone, Monique walked quickly into Kady's room, saying the words, "Hi, Debbie," before she shut the door.

Five minutes later, Monique hurried into the living room. "Sorry about that. So, as I started to say, where are we going to eat tonight? Pick someplace special because it'll be our last dinner together. Debbie just told me to write a wrap-up story by early tomorrow and that'll probably be the one they use in next week's paper. Then I'll pack up and be outta here before tomorrow night."

—m—

Monique liked Edgar's suggestion –The Lobster's Tail, a popular seafood restaurant on the outskirts of town. "A fish place," she said, nodding her approval. "Very appropriate for my last dinner with you."

The three of them slid into Monique's car and she drove to the small freestanding building, which was hard to miss: One outside wall was decorated with a gigantic painting of a lobster with two enormous claws and an oversized tail. Despite not having reservations, a hostess ushered Kady, Monique, and Edgar into the cozy dining room and gave them a booth.

"It's not real crowded here," Kady said, glancing around.

"Probably because it's Thursday night, not Friday or Saturday," her father pointed out.

They opened their menus and examined the lengthy list of entrees. "The prices are very high," Edgar said. "Maybe we should go somewhere else."

"Don't worry about the money," Monique said. "Just order anything you like. This is our final dinner and I've got an expense account, remember?"

Edgar and Monique decided to order the restaurant's specialty— lobster tails—and Kady chose the red snapper.

"I wonder how long we'll have to be without the lake," the girl said, closing her menu.

"I don't know," Monique said. "It may be a while."

"Poor fish." Edgar shook his head. "All of them have to die. Flung through a pipe and just tossed away like garbage."

They sat quietly until Kady spoke. "You know," she said. "I'm sorry, but I don't really feel like eating seafood tonight. It's like we're celebrating and meanwhile, all those fish in the lake are going to die."

Monique lowered her menu. "I'm starting to agree with you. Suddenly, a lobster dinner doesn't sound so good."

Edgar stood. "Let's find another kind of restaurant," he suggested.

They apologized to the hostess and left The Lobster Tail. Driving through town, they noticed a small Mexican restaurant and stopped there for dinner.

—⚏—

After the fishless meal, which they all enjoyed, Monique drove Edgar home. Then she and Kady returned to town for their shopping expedition. "I found this place earlier today," Monique said as she parked the Elantra and led the girl to a store with flashing colored lights that occupied the middle of a row of small boutique-like shops. "It's called Teens Be-Wear. Ever hear of it?"

"Yes." Kady stared at the autumn-themed windows. "But I've never gone in. I don't buy clothes much."

"It's got some cool shit," Monique said. "C'mon, let's go take a look."

The pulsating sounds of a current hip-hop song greeted them as they entered the little shop. Rows of jeans and tops filled the interior, each headed by a teen girl or boy mannequin dressed in a trendy outfit.

"What about bathing suits?" Kady asked. "Though, with the lake gone, I probably won't be wearing them much now anyway."

"It's late in the season so bathing suits are gonna be dumped in the 'Clearance' section somewhere in the back of the store. We can check them out later." She gave Kady's arm a gentle tug and maneuvered the girl towards an aisle filled with long-sleeve shirts. "We'll start here."

"But it's summer," Kady complained. "This is fall stuff."

"We're working on a school wardrobe. I want you looking good in September."

"What about things I can wear now?"

"That stuff'll be in 'Clearance' too. Real cheap. But first we're gonna pick out some school clothes."

Monique had Kady try on several tops and the girl chose three they both liked. Then they found two pairs of jeans. Finally, Monique led Kady to the back of the store. "Here's the 'Sale' section," she said, pointing to four overstuffed racks of clothes with a sign that read "Reduced up to 90%!" After sifting through the discounted items, Kady selected two bathing suits marked 75% off and three short-sleeve tops, each half-price.

Kady tried on every item of sale clothing without saying anything.

"So?" Monique asked after the girl had finished.

"They all look good." Kady frowned as she zipped up her old jeans and stared at herself in the changing room mirror.

"What the hell's wrong with that?"

"It's too much money. I can't afford all this." The teen waved at the large pile of clothes she liked.

"Well, you have to get the stuff that's on sale," Monique said, holding up one of the bathing suits. "This shit is practically free. Won't your babysitting cover the fall clothes?"

Kady lifted each of the non-sale items she planned to buy and checked its price. "I guess I can do it if I just get two of the shirts." She picked up a pink floral tee. "I don't like this one as much as the others anyway."

Monique charged the clothes on her credit card and she and Kady walked out of the store, each carrying a large shopping bag.

"I'll pay you back as soon as I get the money from Todd's mother."

"I know you..." Monique's phone rang before she could finish her sentence and she checked the number. "Shit! It's my mama. I never called her back." She glanced at Kady. "Listen, I gotta talk to her. Just wait right here and I'll try to make it fast." Leaving her shopping bag on the floor, she flipped open the phone, and ran towards the car.

—ɯ—

As Kady picked up the heavy shopping bag Monique had dropped and began moving it closer to where she stood, she was tripped from behind, her knee hitting the pavement.

"How very clumsy of you," a girl's voice teased.

Looking up from the ground, Kady stared into the smirking face of Hannah Evans. "Gotta watch where you're walking, Fraidy Kady. Why'd you fall down? Just clumsy, or did you see a bug again and freak out?" Hannah pulled back her outstretched leg after first making sure Kady had seen it.

Quickly glancing around, Kady noticed Monique leaning on her car and facing the street while she talked on the phone and Hannah's mother standing a half block behind them, chatting loudly with another woman. There was no one to rescue her. She rose slowly, trying her hardest to picture a piece of toilet paper hanging from Hannah's behind.

"You're way too poor to shop there," Hannah said, pointing to the Teens Be-Wear logo on the shopping bags. "Did *she* buy the clothes for you?" The girl nodded towards Monique, who was having an animated discussion and still facing the other direction.

"No. I get paid for babysitting, so I've got..."

"Who's the black bitch anyway?" Hannah asked, interrupting her explanation.

"Monique's not a bitch!" Kady said emphatically. "She's my friend, a reporter who's staying with me."

"Oh, she's sleeping in your house," Hannah sneered. "Then she's screwing your father." She rolled her eyes dramatically. "How pathetic."

Kady stared at the girl in amazement. "How can you say such awful lies?"

Hannah giggled. "You are such a dumb baby, Fraidy Kady. You probably think..."

"Hannah!"

The girl turned at the sound of her name being called. Hannah's mother, now standing by herself, gestured with an impatient hand signal that she wanted her daughter to join her.

"Sorry we can't talk any more, Fraidy Kady. It's been fun, but Mom's calling so I gotta go." Hannah paused and emphatically shook her head up and down. "Oh, that's right. You don't have a mother. Your mother didn't like you, so she ran off and left you behind." She pointed her forefinger at Kady. "You wouldn't understand anything about having a mom."

Kady was speechless—too stunned and upset to come back with a clever retort. Then she saw Monique close the phone and look at her quizzically, hands on hips.

As Hannah turned to leave, Kady reached out and grabbed the girl's arm. "No!" she shouted. "I'm not listening to your horrible lies anymore!"

Hannah stared at Kady, a frightened look replacing her smug expression. "My mother's calling me," she said quietly.

"Your mother can wait. I have some things to say to you first. I don't know why you have to be so mean—to say and do such awful things to me when I've never done anything bad to you."

"Let go," Hannah muttered, trying unsuccessfully to release Kady's grip.

"No. It's my turn to talk. I'm not going to hurt you now, but if you ever say anything bad about me, my father, or my friends..." She nodded towards Monique, who stood near the car, watching the scene, a huge grin on her face. "...I'll punch you right in the mouth. Understand?"

Hannah wrenched her arm free, rubbed it, and nodded at Kady. Then, without saying a word, she raced towards her mother.

Monique, still smiling, approached Kady. "I guess that must've been the famous Hannah."

Kady nodded.

"She didn't look real happy."

"She was so scared, I think she was about to cry. I did what you said and told her to leave me alone."

"How did it feel?"

"It was hard at first and my heart was beating real fast." Kady smiled broadly. "But then it felt really good."

"So what'd she say this time?" Monique asked as she picked up one of the shopping bags.

"Oh, the usual about how I'm poor and that my mother ran away because she didn't want me...And she called you a black bitch."

"Really?"

Kady glanced at the pavement as she walked to the car. "And then she said you were having sex with my dad."

Monique took a deep breath and let it out slowly. "That girl really knows how to dish it." She squeezed Kady's shoulder. "I'm so proud that you were finally able to fight back and kick ass...Girl's a real chicken, huh?"

"Yeah. And I always thought she was so tough."

"Bullies are usually the biggest scaredy-cats. Strange, isn't it?"

"Very," Kady said, nodding.

"You okay now?"

"Yeah. But I'm still shaking a little...Look." She held out her unsteady hand.

"Must be all that adrenaline," Monique muttered as she unlocked the trunk and stashed the two shopping bags inside. Then she and Kady stepped into the Elantra.

"How about your mother?" the girl asked, attaching her seatbelt. "Is everything all right?"

"I hope." Monique shrugged as she turned on the ignition. "Mama was mad at me 'cause I forgot my sister's birthday. I tried telling her that I was in the middle of a major story here about a killer fish. So she says, 'You got time to think about a damn fish, but not about Chantell?'" The reporter sighed. "I guess she has a point."

She and Kady chuckled as Monique drove to the Gonzalez's house.

—ɯ—

Edgar sat in the living room watching TV when Kady and Monique walked into the cottage, each carrying a large shopping bag. "Looks like you two ladies did well," he said.

"Yeah, we really did—and not just in the store." Monique lowered her bag and turned towards a beaming Kady. "While I was on the phone, that girl Hannah came along and started talking trash again. But, this time, Kady handled it just fine. I don't think Hannah'll be bothering her again."

Edgar rushed to his daughter and put his arm around her. "Really, Kady? That's wonderful!"

"I was scared at first, Dad," she said, hugging him. "But it feels real good now."

"What did you say to her?"

"I told Hannah to stay away from me or I'd hit her."

He smiled and kissed Kady gently on her cheek. "I'm so proud of you." Then he turned to his guest. "Do you want to relax now and watch something?" He indicated the TV.

"No, thanks," Monique said. "I have to start working on my wrap-up article. I promised Debbie I'd get it to her early tomorrow."

"And I'm gonna go to my room and write some more of my story."

They each picked up a shopping bag and entered Kady's room.

"Let me read your article first," the girl said.

"The one I wrote this afternoon about the poison? It's already out of date."

"I don't care. I still want to see it."

"Fine." Monique walked to the desk and turned on her laptop.

Sitting at the desk, Kady read quickly. "Good stuff," she said when she had finished. "Too bad tomorrow will be your last story." She flopped onto her bed.

"Yeah and too damn bad it's ending like this," the reporter said, settling into the desk chair. "I'm glad you finally took care of Hannah, but sorry there's no lake for you and no fish for me."

After taking her notebook and pencil from the drawer next to the bed, Kady propped herself on her stomach. Then, turning to "Mean Girls," she began writing.

"You've got to look where you're going," Anna said. She laughed at Kathy, who was lying on the ground.

"Why'd you hurt me?" Kathy asked. "I never did anything to you." She looked at the trickle of blood running down her knee.

"Because I can. It doesn't matter what I say or do to you, you never do anything about it — and you never will..."

"Oh yeah?" Kathy said. "You're so wrong. I'm going to tell you just what I think of you — you mean, awful girl."

And she did.

CHAPTER 22

TOWN WILL DESTROY PEACHWOOD LAKE TO KILL MONSTER FISH!

by Monique Atchison

PEACHWOOD, CONNECTICUT — This town has given up the fight. On Thursday, it conceded defeat to the mysterious fish that has held Peachwood Lake hostage for nearly two weeks.

Police equipped with Tasers and divers carrying spear guns couldn't kill the murderous creature. Even a bomb blast failed. And Nervirula, a specially-designed poison, didn't work either, although the toxin did slaughter other shelled animals in the water, including many unfortunate turtles.

Admitting she and the Town Board had run out of ideas for ridding the lake of the killer fish, Mayor Margaret Turnbull announced that Peachwood would now take a "drastic" step: dredging the lake. On Saturday morning, the town will begin draining the water out of the lake. This procedure will, of course, kill the armor-plated jumping fish. Sadly, however, this solution will also kill all the other creatures that live in Peachwood Lake, as well as destroy all the aquatic plant life. And in the process, the town will lose its crystal-clear lake...

Monique mentioned the mayor's apology for taking such "extreme action," summarized the information she had learned about the ferocious ancient fish, and then described all six of the Peachwood Lake deaths in great gory detail. It was her last story and Debbie would edit it for Monday's paper edition too. *Gotta let it all hang out.* Monique started to email the article, but then stopped and reached for her cell phone.

—🐛—

"What's all that noise outside?" Todd asked Friday morning as he and Kady sat at the Cimino's kitchen table, playing a game of war. The boy threw down his cards and ran to the back door.

"Wait for me!" Kady yelled, rushing after him. He was already standing at the edge of the water staring to his far right when Kady, breathing heavily, caught up to him.

"Look!" He pointed to Fairview Day Camp. "What're they doing over there?" On the sandy beach, a large truck—equipped with a crane—was noisily lowering a machinery-filled barge into Peachwood Lake.

"That must be a special boat for draining the lake," Kady said, still gasping. "You do know that they're taking out all the water tomorrow?"

"Yeah. My dad told me." The boy turned to Kady. "Will that kill the jumping fish so it's dead?"

She nodded. "It's still a fish so it can't live if it doesn't have any water to swim in."

"What about all the other fish in the lake?"

"They won't be able to live either."

"Oh." Todd lowered his head, but didn't speak.

As they continued to watch, the barge hit the water with a heavy splash and a man immediately tethered it to the dock. Then two other workers hauled several large pieces of black pipe onto the beach and placed them next to the barge.

"What's that stuff for?" Todd asked.

"I think they're gonna set up a long pipe to get rid of bigger things in the lake that can't be drained," Kady explained.

"Like all the fish?"

The girl bobbed her head in agreement.

Clutching her cell phone, Monique stood up.

"Hello," said a voice behind her.

The reporter turned and stared at Pete Malone. "How long have you been here watching me?" she asked.

"A while." The police officer sat directly behind the desk at which Monique had been working. "But you were so caught up in your writing that I didn't want to disturb you."

"Why are you here anyway?" She put her hands on her waist and grinned. "Did I break some kind of town law?"

Pete returned her smile, his hazel eyes twinkling. "Well, I kind of figured you'd be leaving soon, now that this fish story's just about over, so I wanted to see you again to say goodbye."

"How'd you even know I'd be here?"

"You told me that you write your stories in the library." He grinned again. "I'm a cop, remember? It's my job to follow clues."

Monique chuckled. "Yeah, as a matter of fact, I'm packing up and heading home this afternoon." She sat down, turning her chair so she faced him. "It was nice of you to stop by and thanks again for your help the other night. I'm real glad I got to meet you."

"Same here." Pete leaned back in his seat and shrugged. "Sorry we didn't have a chance to get to know each other better...You planning on ever coming back to Peachwood?"

Monique nodded. "I'll be visiting Kady, that's for sure."

"Maybe we could get together then—have dinner, see a movie." He pointed to her oversized bag. "You've still got my card, right?"

"Yup."

"Call me when you're in Peachwood."

"Okay, I'll do that."

Pete tilted his head. "So where do you live?"

"Brooklyn."

"I get into the city every once in a while...Got a number I can reach you at?"

"Sure." Monique rummaged through her leather bag. "Here's my card. You can always get me on my cell."

Pete put the business card in his shirt pocket and stood. "Well then, I guess it's goodbye for now." Awkwardly, he held out his right hand.

Monique rose and shook the outstretched hand. "Yeah," she said, smiling softly. "I guess it is."

—⟋⟋⟍—

"C'mon, Todd," Kady said. "Nothing's happening out here anymore. Let's go back inside...Afraid I'm gonna beat you?" She smiled at the boy.

Todd ignored her challenge. "They're still carrying all that pipe stuff to the beach," he said, pointing to the workers scurrying around Fairview Day Camp like busy ants.

"But it's boring standing here just watching men stack pieces of pipe." Kady held out her hand. "Besides, it's starting to rain. We should go in and finish our game."

"Okay, but I wanna come back out later," Todd said as he began walking towards his house.

Kady fell into step with him. "Why?" she asked.

"Maybe they'll do something else more exciting."

"They're only setting up equipment today. They're not going to start working on draining the lake till tomorrow."

"I still wanna watch."

"All right, as long as it's not raining."

Todd stopped in front of the sliding glass door and turned to Kady. "Mommy said I'm starting a new camp next week."

"Oh." It was sooner than Jill had said; it wasn't even August yet. *Less money*, Kady thought as she tried to hide her disappointment. "She didn't tell me."

"It's called Camp Kiddeo," the boy continued. "Kinda a dumb baby name, don't you think?"

"The name's not important, as long as the camp's fun."

"Mommy says I can go swimming there," he said, opening the door and walking inside. "It's got a pool, not a lake."

"Then there'll be no bad fish to worry about." Kady followed Todd into the house and closed the back door.

—⟋⟍—

After she watched Pete leave the library, Monique went to a nearby alcove next to an unoccupied table and made a call. The phone was answered on the second ring. "Hi, Frank," she said. "It's Monique. You didn't call me, but I'm just checking in to see if there's anything new."

"Not really," the scientist said. "I'm sorry, Monique."

"I'm writing my final story on the fish, kind of a wrap-up, and I just wanted to make sure I'm not missing something." She hesitated briefly. "What went wrong with that Nervirula shit yesterday?"

Frank sighed. "What a disaster! The tests on Nervirula were a hundred percent effective. The research team assured us that the toxin would work."

"Yeah. Tell that to all the dead turtles."

"I know, I know. Animal-rights groups have been calling us nonstop—screaming on the phone—since it happened. The Ecological Protection Patrol is circulating a petition online, demanding that the state cut our research funding. It's a madhouse here."

"Anything else about the fish?"

"Well, we're just about positive it's not a known species, so it's either something entirely new or some sort of mutation. But we won't be able to figure it out unless we can examine the fish."

"Are you guys going to try to find it when they pump the lake?"

"We're trying to work out a plan. They're directing the pipeline to a town-owned lot not too far from Peachwood Lake. But we'll probably have to dig through mountains of dead fish and vegetation, and if we can't find it quickly, the seagulls and other predators will ruin it for us."

"Yucch! Sounds smelly."

"It will be, that's for sure."

"Okay, then I'm going to add a line to my story about the possibility that the fish could be a new species. Is that all right with you?"

"It's fine. Just don't use my name or mention Connecticut State Labs."

"You're still my 'scientific expert involved in the case.'"

"That works...Sorry I don't have more for you."

"And I'm sorry this story's got such a shitty ending. Thanks for your help, Frank."

Monique tossed the phone into her bag, returned to her laptop, and wrote: "Scientists have determined the killer fish is not a member of any known species. One scientific expert involved in the case thinks it could be an entirely new kind of fish." After inserting the two sentences into her article, Monique emailed it to Debbie. Then she turned off her computer and left the library.

In the middle of the afternoon, Todd's doorbell rang. Looking through the peephole, Kady saw Monique smiling at her. "Hi," she said, opening the door with Todd standing next to her. "What's up?"

Monique pointed to her bright red car, parked next door at

Kady's house. "I'm all packed and ready to leave, so I'm just here to return your key and say goodbye."

"Oh." Frowning, the girl lowered her head. "That's right. You did say you were going home today."

"Yeah, I finished my story and they're draining the lake tomorrow, so now it's time for me to go." She reached over and gently lifted Kady's head. "Hey, what happened to last night's smiley face? Thought you were done with all the frowning, girl. Makes you look damn ugly!"

"That's not ugly," Todd said. "Look at this." He made a contorted face, puckering his lips and squinting his eyes.

Kady smiled. "That is pretty gross."

"And you're pretty funny," Monique said, rumpling the boy's blond hair. Turning to Kady, she handed her the house key and a small wrapped box with a bow on top. "Here. This is for your dad."

The girl examined the package. "What is it?"

"Just a little something for letting me stay with you two this past week," she said, kissing Kady softly on the cheek. "I'll talk to you soon and, don't forget, you can always call me."

"When will you be coming back?"

"I don't know, but I'll be in touch. You got to keep me up to date on what's going on with the lake."

"Sure." Kady nodded her head and tried to smile.

"Hey, you're my junior reporter so call me if anything new happens." Then, with a wave, Monique turned and headed to her Elantra.

CHAPTER 23

"Shit! No messages." Rachel Castell turned off her BlackBerry and grumbled to herself as she walked out of McDonald's after drinking yet another cup of black coffee.

It's not fair, she thought, getting into her silver Toyota Corolla and slamming the door. Her rage had been steadily building since six o'clock the previous night when she abruptly left the news desk after Mayor Turnbull's announcement that the town would be dredging Peachwood Lake.

Rachel hadn't slept or eaten since then. A few minutes ago, she had ordered a Big Mac. But just looking at it on her tray had made her nauseous and she had tossed the uneaten burger into the garbage. *How the hell can I eat—and why should I?* She leaned back in the seat and closed her eyes.

Rachel had expected her extensive coverage of the killer-fish story to be her big break. She had the whole scenario planned out: Some network honcho in New York City was supposed to see her work on TV and say to an assistant, "That girl is going to be a huge star! Hire her!" But, so far, it hadn't happened.

Why not? She clenched her teeth as she opened her eyes and clutched the steering wheel. She was young and smart, she looked great on camera, and everyone said she was "going places."

Until the jumping fish appeared, all the news stories Rachel had covered for WBTR-TV were the typical ho-hum small town stuff—an occasional robbery, fire, domestic dispute. But this one was different. It was her opportunity. She was destined to move up to a network job; it was her time, and she was ready. The Peachwood Lake story was her calling card—only no one was calling.

And tomorrow they were draining the damn lake. *End of fish story. End of network job...*

"No!" she yelled out loud, punching the steering wheel with both hands. "It's not ending like that! I can't let it end that way!" After her outburst, Rachel sat quietly for a few minutes. Then, feeling slightly better, she started the car and drove to a nearby store.

After Monique left, Todd tugged on Kady's arm. "Let's go back outside and see what's going on at the lake," he said.

"It's boring. Nothing's going on."

"You promised!"

Kady sighed. "Okay. But if they're just carrying more stuff to the beach, I don't want to watch."

Todd ran out the back door, with Kady following. She reached the boy and gazed at the water, which was still littered with the corpses of many turtles. Todd pointed to the Fairview Day Camp beach, now filled with piles of long black pipes. "The men left," he said.

"I told you. They're not doing anything with the lake till tomorrow. C'mon. There's nothing to see here."

Slowly, Todd and Kady walked back into the house.

Rachel Castell paid the cashier and left the sporting goods store. After placing her purchases in the trunk of the car, she drove to Peachwood Lake.

"Good, no one's here," she mumbled as she parked the Corolla in the Fairview Day Camp parking lot, opened the trunk, and removed the two items she had just bought.

Shaking her head angrily, the newscaster maneuvered around the stacks of pipes on the beach until she reached the lake. "Can't let 'em do this!" she muttered as she reached the barge tethered to the dock and kicked it. *F___ing dredge boat! It'll ruin everything!*

Across from the barge, several of the camp's rowboats floated in the water, pairs of oars on the bottom of each boat. Rachel stepped into one of the boats and untied it from the pier. Then, placing the oars in the oarlocks, she began rowing steadily towards the middle of Peachwood Lake.

—◊◊—

"I wanna go back outside!" Todd yelled, jumping up from his chair in the kitchen.

"We were just out and nothing's happening," Kady argued. "No one's even at the camp anymore." She glanced at the window. "Besides, it looks like it's starting to rain again."

"But I don't wanna play checkers. It's no fun!" The boy pushed the game board aside, knocking some of the discs onto the floor. "Let's play soccer. I'll go get the ball." He rushed out the door without waiting for a response.

"Only if it's not raining!" Kady yelled. After picking up the checkers on the floor, she went outside too.

"See, it's not raining," Todd said, looking up at the sky and holding out his hand when Kady reached him.

"All right," she agreed, running to the middle of the backyard. "Go ahead and kick the ball to me."

After kicking the ball, the boy raced towards Kady to prevent her from returning the kick. But she got to the ball first and booted it near the water. Todd ran to retrieve the ball.

"Don't go into the lake!"

"I know," he muttered as he approached the ball and prepared to kick it again. "I'm little, but I'm not dumb." When his foot touched the ball, he heard a splashing sound so he stopped and gazed at the water. "Look!" he shouted. "Someone's rowing in the lake!"

Kady ran to Todd and stared at the red-haired woman in a boat. "Oh my God. What's she doing?" The teen waved her hands frantically. "Get out of the lake!" she shouted as loudly as she could. "It's dangerous!"

—ɯɯ—

Rachel heard some commotion on the shore. When she turned towards the noise, she saw two children—a girl and a small boy—shouting and waving at her. But she was too far away to understand what they were saying.

Two of my young fans! They even recognize me here! She lowered the oars into the boat and returned their waves. Thinking her fans might want to take her picture, the TV reporter rowed a little closer to them, glad that despite not eating or sleeping she was, as always, appropriately dressed for a photo op. Rachel rested the oars inside the boat, patted her hair, straightened her frilly white blouse, smoothed the crease of her navy slacks, and smiled.

Then, remembering her purpose for being in the lake, she picked up the large hunting knife and net she had just purchased and waited for the jumping fish. "I'm ready for you," she muttered. "I'll catch you, save the lake, and then they'll all want to hire me. It'll be a bidding war..."

Her daydream was interrupted by a splash behind the boat. Turning quickly, she caught sight of a silvery blur as the armored fish reentered the water. Rachel grasped her knife tightly and made sure the net was nearby.

—ɯɯ—

"The fish!" Todd screamed, pointing at a ripple in the water. "It's right behind her!"

"I don't know what she's doing," Kady mumbled, grasping

Todd by the shoulders. "I need you to run into the house, pick up the phone, and press the numbers '911.' Tell them what's happening here. Then stay inside and wait for the police...Don't come out!"

"But I wanna see..."

"Todd, for once, please listen to me without arguing...Call 911. Go now! I really need you to do this."

"Okay."

Kady heard the boy's footsteps as he raced to the house, but she kept her eyes focused on the woman in the rowboat.

The fish jumped again, this time to the woman's right and Kady saw her turn towards the splash. The fish was playing with her, Kady realized. *Like it's some kind of crazy game.*

The rowboat bounced gently in the water, drifting closer to where she stood and Kady could see the woman's face more clearly. "It's that TV reporter, Rachel Castell," she murmured. "Why is she out there?"

She tried screaming again. "Miss Castell, please row back to shore!"

The woman smiled at her, said something, blew a kiss, and waved.

"Oh God!" Kady mumbled, sitting on the grass. "Is she nuts?"

———※———

Rachel heard the girl on the shore call her name. "I love you too!" the newscaster replied. Then she went back to looking for the fish. There was another loud splash and, this time, the bony-plated creature jumped directly in front of her. She saw its huge jagged teeth open and close like a pair of gigantic serrated scissors preparing to cut.

"Come on, you son of a bitch!" Rachel yelled as the fish dove back into the water. "You don't scare me! I'm all ready for you!" She clutched the sharp knife.

As if it understood and accepted her challenge, the fish leaped again and launched itself at her face. She turned slightly and the creature latched onto her right cheek and began biting through it with the effectiveness of a surgeon's scalpel.

"Let go!" Rachel screamed, using her knife to repeatedly stab the ferocious fish. But the blade didn't penetrate the animal's bony armor and the creature kept chewing through the flesh on her face.

"Noooo!" Rachel yelled, tossing the knife away and trying to use both hands to pry off the fish. But it had latched on too tightly and continued to methodically gnaw through her bloodied cheek, advancing upwards, towards her eye.

—ɯ—

The rowboat had been drifting towards Kady and was only about fifty feet away when she saw the fish attack the newscaster. Jumping up, the teen kicked off her sandals, dove into the water, and swam quickly to the boat.

Climbing inside, she saw Rachel writhing on the floor of the boat trying to free herself from the fish's unyielding grip. The right side of the woman's face was a mass of pulpy, bloody flesh and her eye had been ripped out of its socket and dangled loosely nearby. Kady told herself not to look and turned away before she threw up.

Grabbing an oar, the girl tried to poke the fish. But the stick had no effect as the creature continued its violent march up Rachel Castell's face. Kady thought quickly. *It's a fish...Needs water. Get it out of the lake.* Putting the oars back into the water, she rowed as fast as she could to Todd's backyard.

Kady jumped out of the rowboat and shoved it onto the grass. Then she rushed to Rachel Castell. Although the woman was no longer moving, the fish continued to feast on the flesh on her forehead.

Trying to get the monster off Rachel, the girl picked up the net, still lying on the bottom of the boat, and waved it at the fish. The creature released Rachel and chomped at the net, ripping the mesh in half with one quick bite. Then, seeming to notice Kady for the first time, the fish lunged at her bare left leg.

"Oww!" The girl jumped off the boat with the fish still attached to the middle of her leg. Moaning in pain, Kady struggled to move as the fish continued chewing her. A few feet away, she saw a large rock. Hopping to the stone, she picked it up, and, with all her strength, smashed the rock on top of the creature's armored head. The fish let go of her leg, dropped to the ground, and stared at her. Then, opening its mouth and flashing enormous jagged teeth—now stained a bright red—the fish moved slightly towards the lake, seemingly trying to use its pelvic fins like feet.

"A walking fish?" Kady mumbled. "Oh no you don't." She took the rock and pounded the squirming creature over and over again. Finally, the fish fell back onto the grass and lay there, motionless. Kady, gasping heavily, was still holding the stone when she heard the shrieks of sirens, getting louder and louder.

—⟋⟍—

"Kady! The police are here!" Todd yelled as he ran up to her. "I did what you said."

"Thanks." She let the rock slip out of her hand and put her wet arm around the boy.

"You're bleeding, Kady," Pete Malone said, reaching them and pointing to the girl's leg.

Glancing down, she saw the blood oozing from the fish's powerful bites. "Yeah," she said quietly as she started to feel dizzy. "Maybe I'm gonna sit." Slowly, she lowered herself to the grass.

Pete turned around and waved his arms. "Hurry! We need medical assistance over here!" Two EMT workers rushed towards them.

"I'll be okay," Kady said. "My leg can wait." She nodded towards the beached rowboat. "Tell them to check the woman in the boat first. It's the TV reporter, Rachel Castell, and she's in real bad shape."

Hearing Kady's words, the young woman and older man carrying medical supplies dashed to the rowboat.

"Kady's a hero!" Todd said to Pete, who knelt on the ground holding his hand against Kady's leg to stop the flow of blood. "She killed the bad fish dead." The boy pointed to the huge-toothed silver-plated creature on the ground next to them.

The policeman stared at the dead fish. "Don't touch it," he said. "We've got to get the fish to the scientists so they can study it."

"She beat up the bad fish," the boy continued. "Pow! Pow! Pow!" He pretended to pound an invisible object with his fists. "I saw her do it."

"I thought you said you listened to me and stayed inside."

"I called the police number like you said. But then I waited outside and watched what happened." Todd turned to Pete. "She swam to the rowboat to help the lady."

The officer shook his head. "You could have been killed."

Kady shrugged as he continued to press his hand on her wound, ignoring the drops of water from her wet hair and soggy shirt that splashed his arm.

The male EMT returned to Kady's side, relieved Pete, and began working on her injured leg. "The cut's too big and jagged," he explained to the policeman. "It needs to be stitched."

Pete took out his cell phone, and faced Kady. "I'm calling your dad to let him know what happened and to meet us at the hospital."

"Thank you," she said. "And then please call Monique and tell her to come back here. She's gonna have a better ending for her story."

CHAPTER 24

WEIRD WORLD WEEKLY EXCLUSIVE!
**1st INTERVIEW WITH KADY GONZALEZ,
PEACHWOOD LAKE HEROINE!**

WWW reporter Monique Atchison spoke with Kady Gonzalez on Friday, immediately after the 13-year-old girl killed the monster fish that had been terrorizing her Connecticut town.

WWW: *Kady, why did you go into Peachwood Lake?*

KG: The boy I was babysitting, Todd [Todd Cimino, age 6] and I were playing soccer when we saw a woman in a rowboat. We tried yelling to her to go back to shore, but she didn't listen to us.

WWW: *Do you think she didn't hear you?*

KG: I don't know. Maybe. But she must have heard something, because she turned around and waved to us.

WWW: *The woman turned out to be Rachel Castell, a local TV reporter. You recognized her?*

KG: Not at first. But, after the boat drifted closer, I did.

WWW: *You told Todd to call the police?*

KG: Yes, when we saw the fish jump.

WWW: *That's when you went into the water although the police were on their way? You knew it was very dangerous.*

KG: I already saw one person die in the lake. [Martin Urloch, 68, Kady's neighbor and the fish's first victim]. I couldn't just stay there and do nothing and watch it happen again.

WWW: *What did the fish do?*

KG: First it played with Miss Castell, like a game, jumping all around her. Then it jumped on her face and held on.

WWW: *Is that when you dove into the water?*

KG: Yes.

WWW: *What did you do when you reached the boat?*

KG: I tried to get the fish off of her. I hit it with the oar, but that didn't do anything.

WWW: *What did you do next?*

KG: I knew I couldn't pull the fish off her so I rowed to the shore.

WWW: *Did you have a plan?*

KG: I was trying to get the fish on land, out of the water, so I would have a chance to kill it. I figured it couldn't stay out of the water forever.

WWW: *How was Rachel Castell when all this was happening?*

KG: She was lying on the bottom of the boat. Her face was all messed up...[Kady stops talking and starts to cry.]

WWW: *I'm sorry, Kady. Should we skip this part?*

KG: No, I'll be okay. I just feel so bad that I couldn't save her. I should have jumped into the water sooner.

WWW: *Don't blame yourself, Kady. You did all you could. So you got the rowboat to the shore. And then what happened?*

KG: Then I tried to use the net to get it off her, but the fish just bit through it.

WWW: *That's when the fish jumped on your leg and started chewing it?*

KG: Yes.

WWW: *That must have hurt.*

KG: Yeah, it did. I wanted to get it off me and kill it.

WWW: *What happened next?*

KG: I picked up a big rock and hit the fish hard on its head.

WWW: *Did that work?*

KG: Yes. The fish fell to the ground.

WWW: *Why do you think hitting the fish on its head worked this time, when it didn't work earlier?*

KG: The fish had been out of the water for a long time. It must have been getting weaker.

WWW: *Was it dead after you hit it?*

KG: Not at first. It tried to get up and go back into the lake.

WWW: *What did you do then?*

KG: I kept hitting it hard with the rock.

WWW: *That killed it?*

KG: Yeah, after a while. It finally stopped moving.

WWW: *When did the police and the ambulance*

arrive?

KG: Right after I killed the fish.

WWW: *How is your leg?*

KG: It's okay. I just have a deep cut where the fish bit me and I needed stitches. But I'm fine.

WWW: *Thank you, Kady. Everyone is very proud of you for killing the fish and saving the lake.*

KG: It would have been a lot better if I could have helped Rachel Castell.

For more stories about the monster fish in Peachwood Lake, see pages __, __, and __.

"It's very good," Edgar said as he sat at Kady's desk Friday evening and finished reading the interview on Monique's laptop. Then he turned to his daughter, who rested her injured left leg on the bed, and wagged his finger at her. "But I still can't believe you jumped into the lake and fought with the fish. You could have easily been killed."

"I'm sorry, Dad. I really didn't have time to think about that... But the fish's dead and I'm okay."

"That's not the point," he continued. "I told you to stay out of water and you didn't listen."

"I already apologized," Kady whispered.

"You have to promise that you'll do what I tell you from now on. I'm still your dad—even if you are a famous 'star.'"

"I promise."

"Good." Edgar nodded at her. "Now you can get back to enjoying your fame."

Kady smiled at him and addressed Monique, who sat on the second bed. "What about the other stories?" she asked. "What pages will they be on?"

"I don't know yet. They're using a bunch of my earlier articles plus my revised wrap-up. The editor'll set all that up before *Weird World* is printed."

"It comes out on Monday?" Kady asked.

"Um-hum." Monique nodded. "And this story's not going online before that. The public doesn't get to read it anywhere till Monday."

"Wow!" the girl said as she leaned back on her pillow. "You made me sound like a real hero."

"You are a real hero...And there's something else I haven't told you."

"What?"

"You're getting paid for this story."

"Why?" She gave Monique a puzzled look. "You're my friend so I wanted you to interview me first."

The reporter chuckled. "*Weird World* doesn't have to know that. They always pay for exclusives and this one's no exception." She smiled at Kady and Edgar. "Guess how much?"

"A hundred dollars?" Kady asked.

"How about ten thousand?"

"That much?" The girl let out a deep breath.

Monique nodded.

Edgar looked at her in disbelief, his mouth wide open. "You're serious?" he asked.

"Very."

Edgar smiled at his daughter. "We'll put it in the bank for your college."

Kady was quiet for a moment. "That's great, Dad," she finally said. "But I'd really like to use some of the money for a computer and Internet service. Can I?"

"Sure," he said, nodding his head. "I know a computer's something that all you writers need."

—☽—

Several minutes later, the Gonzalez's phone rang, as it had been doing constantly since late afternoon when they had returned from the hospital. After the first few calls, Kady and Edgar had opted to screen the callers, mostly media types hoping to talk to Kady. But she had spoken to a few people.

She had picked up the phone when Jake Ellsbury, the *County Courier* reporter, began leaving a message. He was thrilled to reach her and had immediately begun asking questions.

"Sorry, I can't talk to you," Kady had interrupted.

"Why not?"

"I don't trust anything you write. You couldn't even spell my name right." Then she had hung up the phone and smiled at Edgar and Monique. "That felt good!"

Kady had also spoken to Mayor Margaret Turnbull, who, after asking how her leg was feeling, offered congratulations for her heroics. "We'd like you to come down to Town Hall one day soon," the mayor had said. "We want to officially honor you for saving Peachwood Lake." Kady's face had turned red as she thanked the woman.

A few minutes later, when someone named Felice Bellway left a message, Monique had asked Kady to return the call.

"Why?" She had given Monique a questioning look.

"Felice is a friend of mine, a reporter/photographer who I met at the day camp. Call her and let her interview you sometime after Monday."

So Kady had spoken to Felice Bellway and made a date to meet with her on Wednesday.

There was one other phone call Kady had answered on Friday: A representative from the "Today" show had asked her to appear on the TV program on Monday. After glancing at Monique, Kady had asked the caller, "Can we make it on Tuesday?" The man had agreed. A limo was going pick her and Edgar up Monday evening; they would spend the night in a Manhattan hotel and be driven to the show in the morning.

"You're a celebrity!" Monique had exclaimed after the call, giving the teen a hug. "How does it feel?"

"Weird—really, really weird." Kady had shaken her head in amazement.

Now, late in the evening, Monique pulled aside the living room curtain and peeked out the window. "Some of the reporters are still there," she said. "I see the TV van and a couple of other cars."

"Will they stay there all night?" Kady asked.

"Who knows?" Monique shrugged. "You're a celebrity and we media people are very persistent...Remember when I called you from that cornfield in Kansas? I sat there in my rental car all night."

"Looking for the UFO."

"Yup."

Edgar settled in front of the TV and Monique dumped the paper plates and empty cartons of Chinese food in the garbage while Kady sat in the upholstered chair, resting her injured leg. The three of them had decided to have food delivered rather than leave the house and risk being mauled by media stalkers. Monique had consented to stay through the weekend to help the Gonzalezes deal with Kady's newfound fame.

"Did I mention that I called Frank this afternoon?" Monique asked Kady as she used a paper towel to pick up some stray pieces of rice from the kitchen table.

"No, you didn't. What did he say?"

"He said he'll let us know what the scientists find out about the fish before they make it public. He'll call me as soon as he knows something."

Monique finished cleaning the table and approached the teen, whose eyes were half closed.

"Girl, you've had it. Been a long day and you kicked some serious ass."

Kady smiled and yawned.

"Go say goodnight to your dad and let's go to sleep."

"That's my yearbook picture," Kady said, leaning over her father's shoulder Saturday morning as he sat at the kitchen table, reading the newspaper.

"You wouldn't let them photograph you yesterday, so that's probably the only picture they could find," Edgar said.

"I let Monique take lots of pictures of me for her story." Kady grinned at her friend and then returned to the article. "At least that reporter spelled my name right this time."

Monique twirled her cereal spoon in the bowl. "Girl, everyone will spell your name right from now on."

Kady smiled as she sat down. "What else does the story say?"

"The town's going to remove the dead turtles and fish from the lake today and take down all the signs," Edgar said, putting the paper aside. "Tomorrow, they're reopening Peachwood Lake."

"Great!" Kady clapped her hands. "There's still lots of summer left."

"It's all thanks to you," Monique said.

In the other room, a phone rang—not the Gonzalez's this time, but the reporter's cell. Monique dashed into Kady's bedroom and returned to the kitchen a short time later. "That was Frank," she said. "He's coming over here now to tell us what they found out about the fish."

—⁂—

A half hour later, the doorbell chimed. Monique peeked outside before opening the door. "It's okay. It's Frank, not a reporter." Quickly, she let him in. "Any news people out there this morning?"

"Just a TV truck," he said. "Someone jumped out and ran after me, asking who I was."

"What did you do?"

"I didn't say anything, just walked faster." After introducing himself to Edgar, the scientist carried his briefcase to the kitchen table and sat. The others joined him.

"Okay, I figured you guys deserved an in-person account of all this," Frank said. He turned to Kady. "First of all, congratulations for not only killing the fish, but also for saving it for us so that we could identify it."

She smiled softly and nodded.

"Have they released any pictures of the fish?" Monique asked.

"No. I don't think so."

"Good. That's another exclusive for me." Pete had allowed her to photograph the creature before sending it to the lab.

"All right. Here goes." Frank opened his briefcase, took out two pictures and placed one on the table. "If you remember, this is the Coccosteus, the prehistoric fish that's been extinct for millions of years," he said to Kady and Monique.

The girl pointed to the drawing. "It had bony plates instead of teeth, but they were really big and sharp."

"That's right," Frank said. "Good memory. Also, it had armor, but only over the front of its body." He placed a photo next to the drawing. "This is the fish that Kady killed yesterday. Notice that it's got armor all over its body. And check its mouth. Those are real teeth, not plates."

"So what kind of fish is it?" Edgar asked.

"It's something new—a whole new species. We think it must be a mutation that evolved from the Coccosteus."

Monique tapped the photo with her fingers. "Where's it been hiding all these years?"

"Who knows?" Frank said, shrugging. "But it's here now. And there're a couple of other interesting things." He pointed to one of the fish's lower fins. "Can you see something here, a little stub?" The others studied the photo carefully.

"There's something, but it's very small," Monique said.

"We think this jumping fish was developing some sort of rudimentary foot, for walking on land."

Edgar, Monique, and Kady all stared at the scientist.

"Just before I killed it, I thought that it was trying to walk," Kady said. "But how could it do that? It's a fish."

"Yes." Frank nodded. "It is a fish—but a very strange one that already has the ability to jump out of the water, almost like a frog. And here's the other fascinating part: Although you can't see it, when we dissected the creature, we found another similarity to an amphibian. In addition to gills, this fish has a partially-developed lung chamber that allows it to breathe air as well as water." He glanced at Kady. "That's why it was able to survive out of the water for a considerable length of time."

"Jeez." Edgar shook his head. "What a monster!"

"Yeah." Frank tapped the photo. "I guess we're very lucky. Completely developed lungs for breathing air and a pair of fully-formed legs would have made this creature just about invulnerable."

—m—

After Frank left, Monique excused herself. "I'm going to add this new fish info to my wrap-up story."

"Do you have to go to the library?" Kady asked.

"Nah. It's short so I'll just text it to Debbie. She's already got the photos."

Edgar had turned on the TV and Kady was flipping the remote to find a show to watch when their phone rang again. The calls had slowed down considerably since Friday, but they were still fairly frequent. The ringing stopped and she and her father heard a boy's voice begin to leave a message. "Hi, Kady. It's Jared and I just wanted..."

"I'm gonna take this call," Kady said, darting to the kitchen as quickly as her wounded leg allowed.

"Hi, Jared," she said, picking up the phone. "Sorry I didn't answer right away, but we've been getting a lot of calls."

"I'll bet."

"How've you been?"

"I'm good, Kady...Look, I just wanted to tell you how great it was what you did yesterday. You know, with the fish."

"Thanks."

"I mean, after all the crap they tried—the bomb and poison and stuff—you're the one that killed it."

"I was just lucky."

"It was like you were a superhero—you know, Spiderman or

Batman. I guess maybe more like Supergirl..."

Kady changed the topic. "Jared, who do you have for homeroom?"

"Mr. Francisco. Who's your teacher?"

"I have him too. We're in the same homeroom."

"That's cool. I'll see you in a couple of weeks then."

"Yeah. I'll see you in school."

"Great. Bye, Kady."

"Bye, Jared. Thanks for calling." She smiled as she hung up the phone.

Kady didn't venture outside on Saturday. Her leg still hurt and the TV van remained parked in front of the house. In the afternoon, Edgar and Monique went grocery shopping and, after they unpacked all the bags, Monique offered to pick up dinner.

"What would you two like?"

"How about pizza?" Kady suggested.

"Fine with me," Edgar said.

"Okay, I'll go to that place in the mall that you like...But then I'm going out."

"Where to?" the girl asked.

"I'm seeing a movie with Pete Malone."

"A date?" Kady asked, grinning.

"Sort of, I guess." Monique shrugged.

When she returned to the Gonzalez's cottage in the middle of the night, Kady was sound asleep.

"How was your date?" the girl asked the next morning.

"Fine." Monique smiled, but didn't elaborate.

"Are you seeing him again?"

Monique just nodded.

Kady, Edgar, and Monique spent a quiet Sunday together. Although it was the "on week" for church, Kady and her father decided not to attend services. "I don't want to be the center of attention there," the teen argued. "Let's go next week instead."

In the afternoon, Kady walked slowly to her dock. She sat, dangling her legs over the clear water, and smiled. Peachwood Lake glistened in the bright sunlight, no dead animals littering its surface. She counted four rowboats and two sailboats and at least twenty swimmers, many of them children because she could hear their laughter and shrieks. On the far right, the Fairview Day Camp beach was empty. The barge, heavy machinery, and black pipes had all been removed.

For Sunday's dinner, the three of them agreed to eat at The Lobster's Tail, the restaurant they had walked out of on Thursday. "Now it's the perfect place," Monique said. "We can call it a 'no-more-killer fish' celebration."

"It's also a goodbye dinner," Kady added. Monique was going home on Monday morning.

—*m*—

Lucky Monique took me to buy some new clothes, Kady thought the following afternoon as she packed for her overnight hotel stay before the "Today" show appearance. The phone rang, and since the media calls had just about stopped—even the TV van was no longer parked in front of the house—Kady hobbled into the kitchen to answer it.

"It's me," Monique said.

"Hi. I was just thinking about you. Is everything okay?"

"Oh yeah. I'm home...Did you read *Weird World*?"

"Dad picked up five copies before he went to work. I read it this morning. The stories are great!"

"Thanks...I have some news."

"Oh."

"I just got a call."

"So...Monique, you're dragging this out. Please tell me!"

"Okay, so this man calls up and introduces himself. He's the Executive Editor of *The New York Times* and he tells me he's been following my work and he just read my exclusive on you and my other fish stories in *Weird World*...Do you believe people at the *Times* read this shit?"

"Monique!"

"Sorry. So he asks me if I want a full-time job with the *Times*' Magazine. Seems they're starting a new column called 'Stranger Than Fiction,' focusing on amazing weird shit, and he thinks I'd be the perfect one to write it."

"What did you say?"

"What do you think I said?"

"Oh Monique, that's wonderful!"

"Listen, I gotta go...Just wanted to tell you the news. Talk to you soon. Remember, I'm coming back to Peachwood next week to help you buy a computer."

"And to see Pete Malone?"

Monique chuckled. "Yeah, well maybe that too."

—⟋⟍—

Kady had finished packing and was working on her short story while she waited for her father to come home from work when the phone rang again.

"Hello," she said.

The line was quiet for a moment. "Kady," a girl's voice said. "It's Bethany. How're you doing?"

"I'm fine."

"That's good...I heard about what you did with the fish. Awesome."

"Thanks."

"Welcome...Umm, I thought maybe we could do something together before school starts, maybe go shopping in the mall or..."

"Aren't you friends with Hannah? I thought I saw you at the pool with her."

"Yeah, I was there. But I'm not friends with Hannah anymore. She was so mean to you and now she's starting in with Caitlin. I'm sorry about what happened and if you don't want to be friends, I can understand, but I..."

"You're not hanging out with Hannah at all anymore?"

"No, I swear...I never liked what she did with you, but, you know..." Bethany's voice drifted off.

"Maybe we can meet at the mall sometime next week," Kady suggested.

"That'd be great. Let me give you my number."

Kady grabbed her pencil and wrote down the information. "Thanks, Bethany. I'll give you a call in a couple of days. Okay?"

"That'll be super."

"Yeah. Thanks for calling. Bye."

Kady hung up the phone and pumped her fist in the air. Then, turning to the page of "Mean Girls" she had been writing, she picked up the pencil.

> *Kathy hit Anna hard in the mouth.*
> *Anna fell to the ground and touched her lip. "I'm*
> *bleeding," she cried. "Why'd you do that?"*
> *"Because you deserve it," Kathy said.*
> *"You're a mean girl and I'm not going to let you*
> *push me around any more." She moved closer to*
> *Anna and waved a fist at her. "And, if you ever*
> *bother me again, I'll hit you harder! Now go!"*
> *Sobbing loudly, without looking back,*
> *Anna jumped up and ran away—forever.*

THE END

Kady put down her pencil, closed the notebook, and smiled.

EPILOGUE
Three Months Later

"Paddle over to the right, Brett."

On a crisp and clear October morning, Paige Sinclair and her husband, Brett, were canoeing on Lake Cicero in New Hampshire. The canoe outing had been Paige's idea. An avid amateur photographer, she wanted to snap some photos of the fall foliage and the view from the lake was simply spectacular.

After Paige took several pictures of trees filled with glorious crimson, gold, and orange leaves, she glanced around the lake to determine where she wanted to go next. Suddenly, the Sinclairs heard a loud splashing noise somewhere behind them.

"What's that?" Paige asked. She and Brett paddled several feet towards the rippling water, held their oars, and waited. Soon they heard a second loud splash and, this time, the Sinclairs saw a long silver fish leap high into the air.

"Awesome!" Brett said. "I've never seen a fish jump in this lake."

"Me neither," Paige added. "Let's paddle closer so, when it jumps again, I can take its picture."

AFTERWARD

As I started writing this novel, I began to wonder if any real fish might have had the ability to terrorize mythical Peachwood Lake. And, when I did the research, a funny thing happened: I discovered that much of what I had conjured up in my imagination actually existed.

Except for the mutated fish and Nervirula, which are both completely fictional, the other scientific information in the book is true: Nasty armored placoderms—Coccosteus and Dunkleosteus—did inhabit lakes in the Connecticut region many millions of years ago. The dinosaur fish known as the coelacanth and the red tide alga are real too.

In essence, my research validates Monique's new column: Truth is often stranger than fiction!